THE ACCIDENTAL
TIME CADET

ALSO BY MEL GILDEN

The Lucky Duck Affair: A Tale of Mystery
The Jabberwock Came Whiffling
Dangerous Hardboiled Magicians
The Planetoid of Amazement
The Return of Captain Conquer

THE ACCIDENTAL TIME CADET

MEL GILDEN

WILDSIDE PRESS

DEDICATION

Hot jets, Clear Ether, and Spaceman's Luck
To Space Cadets Everywhere

ACKNOWLEDGEMENTS

Cover Art: Glen Orbik
Cover Design: Eric Baldwin
Editorial Support: Evelyn Hughes
and Carla Coupe

CONTENTS

FOREWORD

Back in 2006, when the Worldcon of the science fiction field was held in Los Angeles, the guest of honor was to be Frankie Thomas, an actor who had been portraying heroes in the movies since his teenage years. During the 1950s, and most memorably, he played Tom Corbett, Space Cadet on television, attending Space Academy in the world beyond tomorrow, 2350 AD... in the age of the conquest of space! Anyone who had a TV during those days will have no trouble remembering that show and that performance.

Unfortunately, Thomas died shortly before the convention. But in a manner of speaking, he was still able to attend because the people who ran the 2006 Worldcon published a book—edited by Mike Resnick and oddly enough called *Space Cadets*—that would include original short stories featuring the adventures of space cadets. Thomas, the original space cadet, wrote a warm introduction recapping some of his early experiences with Tom Corbett and the other crew members of the good ship *Polaris*.

I was disappointed that I had not been invited to write a story for the *Space Cadets* anthology, but it didn't take me long to decide that there was no reason why I shouldn't write my own space cadet story. *The Accidental Time Cadet* is the result. I tried to include some of the feeling of the original Tom Corbett TV show in it, as well as leavening the story with a more modern kid's book adventure. Only you and the other readers can tell me whether I succeeded.

CHAPTER 1

THE SCOUT SHIP *ROBERT A. HEINLEIN*

Cadet Raymond Hunt stared thoughtfully at the heavy sprinkling of stars contained in the astrogation sphere of the System Guard scout ship *Robert A. Heinlein*. He did his best to ignore the single member of his crew, who was banging around in the galley.

The crewman (who was also chief engineer), Longwood Jan, had been born on Venus, whose terraforming was nearing completion. For some reason Jan was as proud of the local cooking as he was of the major engineering feat. Of course aboard the *RAH* he didn't have access to all the plants and animals that had developed on Venus, seemingly out of nowhere, since the terraforming began: laughing tree buds, scorp sweat, or even that special tasty mud they have in the Weinbaum Swamp, but the grocery computer could do a fair job of assembling ingredients from base molecules. At least that was what Cadet Jan claimed.

Though Hunt knew the *RAH* was travelling pretty fast for a sub-light ship, the green dot representing it in the astrogation sphere seemed to be floating motionless in the center of the infinite universe. At this scale their destination, an asteroid called the Nugget—it had an official serial number, but only astronomers used it and then only when trying to impress each other—was about an inch and a half away. Not far as solar distances went.

While Hunt stared at the display, something crashed in the galley. Hunt shook his head. Jan could have ordered the computer to put the whole meal together, but he insisted on doing it the old-fashioned way.

Hunt spoke to the ship's computer. "Freddy?"

"Yes, sir?" Freddy said. He was always listening and he was very polite. More importantly, he knew how to keep a secret, should that be necessary.

"Freddy, let me see that article about Professor Eignbergen again."

"Yes, sir."

Immediately the universe in the sphere faded to be replaced by a recording of a small man in a white lab coat. He was fat and seemed to be made from white lumps of varying sizes. He apparently enjoyed having his picture taken because he smiled as he waved his hand through the air, leaving behind a wake of dense mathematics that slowly faded. Below the recording was a running ribbon of text that said PROFESSOR EDWARD EIGNBERGEN, A SCIENTIST FOR ALL AGES.

Hunt shrugged. He had viewed the article before. It still did not tell him much that Commandant Cassidy hadn't told him and Jan before the *RAH* had taken off from Earth. Eignbergen was famous and smart and had been living on the Nugget, working alone for the better part of ten years. The article didn't say what he was working on, and Cassidy hadn't told them—it was possible she didn't know herself. Need-to-know was an article of faith in the System Guards. If Hunt was lucky, he and Jan would learn more while they transported Eignbergen from the Nugget back to Earth. Or maybe not. They were out here to pick him up, not to discuss his work. Need to know? Who knew?

Jan floated up to the control deck, looking ridiculous in his cadet uniform and chef's toque. "Dinner?" he offered as he bobbed a little in the open hatchway.

Hunt told Freddy to put the article away and re-establish the astrogation display, then followed Jan back down to the galley, a room that was just big enough for the two of them to sit at a table where a single game of checkers could be played comfortably.

Dinner that evening, ship's time, was crackpot stew, a Venusian favorite. Still determined to do it the old-fashioned way, Jan ladled a serving into each bowl. The stuff did not actually smell bad, but the odor was unusual and flat and brown—if one can imagine a brown smell. It looked like little islands of something surrounded by an oily green liquid. Tiny hairs grew out of the islands. It was the hairs that really bothered Hunt.

Jan raised his spoon, then looked expectantly at the cadet across the table. "Try it," Jan said, as if irritated at having to make the suggestion.

Hunt continued studying the stuff in his bowl, not even sure it was food.

"You're not afraid, are you?" Jan insinuated with a side order of sarcasm.

Hunt said nothing, but sliced off a small corner of one of the islands with the edge of his spoon, and dipped up some of the green liquid. Bravely, he put it into his mouth. The taste wasn't bad exactly, just sort of brown. He swallowed and did his best to smile at Jan. Smiling was hard work.

"Perk up, Ray," Jan said. "You won't be an 18-year-old cadet forever. Someday you'll be admiral of the whole Guard."

"Yes, and with my luck you'll still be cooking for me."

Jan's mouth curled, and he shook a finger in Hunt's direction.

"Sorry," Hunt said before Jan could let fly a barrage of angry words. "This is actually not bad." He ate more of the stew, and promised himself that from now on either he would do the cooking or he would order Freddy to do it. Hunt had made that promise to himself before, but somehow Jan always managed to get to the kitchen before anybody else. Not even Freddy could beat him. It was possible that Jan had adjusted Freddy's clock—he was a good enough engineer—but there was no way to prove it.

"What do you think Dr. Eignbergen is working on?" Hunt asked, changing the subject. It was an old question that Hunt knew interested Jan. Jan often brought it up at meals.

Jan held his hot expression for a moment and then relaxed. "I'm out of ideas," he said. "What do *you* think he's working on?"

"Need to know, Jan," Hunt said. "Need to know."

"That doesn't mean we can't try to guess."

"He's a physicist," Hunt said. "Could be anything: a new weapon, a better brain for Freddy and his kind, a ground transportation system, a communications device."

"Could be," Jan agreed.

They finished dinner and then went about their evening chores. Jan dropped to the power deck to make sure that everything was all right down there while Hunt did the same on the control deck. Hunt checked their course and with Freddy's help made the necessary tiny corrections. Freddy would take care of things while they slept and awaken them in the unlikely event there arose an emergency he couldn't handle.

* * * *

The next morning, Hunt awakened as his blanket evaporated into a lightly scented cloud of Sleep-Away that lifted him gently into consciousness. He felt his skin cooling and freshening. Once he was up, Freddy sprayed a clean uniform onto him and reported that nothing had happened in the night that required Hunt's attention.

Hunt thanked him, and casually went down the uniform checklist. Many useful features were designed into the spray-on uniform, each of them operated using controls in the cuffs of his uniform shirt: communications devices, an emergency life support system, weapons both offensive and defensive, and something called a percepticon, which could sense and keep track of almost any object or physical component. Rarely was there a problem with any of the uniform accessories, and that status continued today.

"How long till we reach the Nugget?" Hunt asked.

"Approximately eighty-seven minutes."

"Very good. What time is it there?"

"Mid-morning."

"Very good," Hunt said again. "Let me talk to Dr. Eignbergen."

Hunt strolled to the galley, where he found Jan already sitting with his elbows on the table and his head resting on one fist. His eyes were half closed and he did not look up when Hunt entered.

"Pancakes, please, Freddy," Hunt called into the air as he sat down. "Good morning, Jan."

"Don't talk dirty," Jan said.

Hunt knew that morning was not Jan's best time of day. "Sorry," Hunt said, and waited for Freddy to make the pancakes appear.

"I have Dr. Eignbergen," Freddy said.

Jan groaned.

"Hold the pancakes, Freddy," Hunt said. "Dr. Eignbergen?"

"Speaking."

"Dr. Eignbergen, this is Cadet Raymond Hunt of the System Guard scout ship *Robert A. Heinlein*. We'll be at your location in about an hour and a half. Will you be ready to go by then?"

"Cadet?" the doctor asked in surprise. He had the voice of a tenor, with the harsh accent of one of the European republics. The voice matched Eignbergen's appearance in the recordings that Hunt had seen.

Jan shook his head.

"Yes, sir," Hunt explained. "Taking you back to Earth is an assignment in our fourth year command lab course. I assure you that we—"

Dr. Eignbergen interrupted him. "Yes, yes, Cadet Hunt. I didn't mean to be insulting. I'm sure that you and your crew know how to fly that ship of yours—the *Heinlein*?"

"Yes, sir."

"I'll be ready," the doctor said, and was suddenly gone, having broken the connection. He left behind faint static that seemed to come from the far side of the universe.

"Seems like a nice enough guy," Hunt said.

"I hope you're right," Jan said. "Three weeks can be a long time on a ship this size."

Hunt ate his pancakes while Jan gradually awakened right there at the table and eventually demanded a plate of sliced skimmers, another Venusian specialty. They were a mottled green.

After breakfast Jan went back down to the power deck, and Hunt went up to the control deck. They were in constant contact with each other and with Freddy. The closer the ship got to the Nugget, the greater care they took with every adjustment they made. Soon a rock stood out from the background of stars. Hunt checked his instruments. That had to be it. "Hang on," he called to Jan.

"I hate it when you say that."

Hunt smiled and watched the astrogation sphere as Freddy made the final approach.

CHAPTER 2

DR. EIGNBERGEN

The *RAH* slowed to a stop relative to the Nugget using delicate blasts from the steering thrusters. When the maneuver was successfully completed, Hunt told Freddy to release the snake, a long tube that would connect the ship to the asteroid. The clamps made a series of satisfying clanks when they contacted the asteroid's airlock and were secured.

Hunt and Jan met at the *Heinlein's* main airlock, cycled through, and swam along the center of the snake, adjusting their idea of up and down as they left the influence of the ship's artificial gravity field and fell into the growing intensity of the field generated by a machine on the asteroid.

The outer hatch of the asteroid's airlock was open when they arrived at the far end of the snake. They went in, the outer door closed, and since the pressure was already about equal, the inner door opened immediately.

"Good morning, gentlemen," said a tall slim robot. Its voice was pleasantly modulated and had a slight upper-class inflection. It was made of metal that had the shine and smoothness of mercury. The robot had no hair, but the outlines of clothing were etched directly onto its skin. It bent easily in all the usual places—seemingly as limber as an eel. "You may call me Number Six."

Jan introduced himself and Hunt. Number Six gave them a mild professional smile. "Follow me, gentlemen," was all it said as it lead them from tunnel to tunnel, all of which were too smooth and straight to be natural. Hunt and Jan occasionally encountered more robots, most constructed to appear vaguely humanoid. A few were no more than mobile boxes with manipulating arms and flashing lights.

Hunt was thoroughly lost by the time they marched through a wide arch, a doorway into what was obviously Dr. Eignbergen's laboratory. Dressed in what might have been the same white coat he'd been wearing in the reference article Hunt had viewed, the doctor was sitting on a stool staring at a cloud of colorful numbers floating before him in a three-dimensional array. He was surrounded by a lot of equipment, much of which Hunt could not identify. He supposed it had something to do with the doctor's work. Hunt wondered how much of it the doctor would want to take with him.

"Doctor—" Hunt started, but stopped when Eignbergen raised one finger in his direction, and with his other hand slid a red five three spaces to the left. Immediately a fanfare blared from somewhere, and the array was replaced by a magnificent display of fireworks. Eignbergen watched the display with delight. "I've been working on that game for almost a month," he said.

"Congratulations, Doctor," Number Six said.

"Thank you. Are we done packing?"

"Yes, Doctor."

"You and a few of the others take my impedimenta to the airlock. I'm sure these gentlemen have ideas where it should be stowed aboard their ship."

Number Six didn't bow to Dr. Eignbergen, but that was its attitude as it backed out of his presence and left the room.

Hunt glanced around. "Will you be wanting to bring all of this?"

Eignbergen contemplated Hunt with placid curiosity. "What if I did?" he asked gently.

"I'd remind you that we have a limited amount of discretionary space aboard our ship."

Eignbergen laughed. "And you would be right, Cadet Hunt." He shook his head. "No. I am leaving this behind. You'll see that I am taking very little."

"Is Number Six coming with us?" Jan asked.

"I hadn't even considered it," Eignbergen said with astonishment. "It is just a robot, like all the others on this asteroid. It kept me company and helped me in my work, but unlike some people," he smiled briefly at Jan, "I do not become attached to machines."

"Me neither," Jan said, and shrugged.

"Shall we go, Doctor?" Hunt suggested.

Dr. Eignbergen nodded, took off his white coat, and wrapped himself in a more formal grass-green jacket that closed up in front without a wrinkle; the green jacket looked a little ragged, as if he'd been wearing it long past its use-by date. Freddy would have to spray him a new one. All part of the service.

When the doctor led them back through the tunnels, he and the robots ignored each other, as if this were just another day and he wasn't going anywhere special. Apparently it was true that he did not become attached to machines, not even machines that had been his only company for ten years.

Number Six and a small crowd of other robots waited at the airlock with a few flat cases and one more that was big enough to hold the torso of one of his robots. Hunt was surprised and relieved that Dr. Eignbergen had told the truth when he assured them that he wasn't bringing much with him. Hunt had no idea what any of the cases contained, but a security field glowed dully around the big one.

Hunt and Jan led the way back through the snake. Dr. Eignbergen swam after them, showing unexpected skill at moving from one gravity field to the other. Number Six and its assistant robots came after with the luggage. Jan went down to the power deck to prepare for departure while Hunt showed Number Six to the storage bay where the big case could be stowed. Dr. Eignbergen kept the flat cases with him in the small cabin where he would be sleeping for the next three weeks. A few minutes later Number Six and the other robots headed back to the Nugget, leaving the *Heinlein's* crew and her passenger alone. Eignbergen barely glanced at them as they left.

"Freddy, say hello to Dr. Eignbergen," Hunt said.

"Welcome, Dr. Eignbergen," Freddy said. "Please let me know if there is anything at all I can do for you."

The doctor accepted Freddy's covert existence easily. Not a surprise considering that he'd been dealing with robots and other artificial life forms for ten years. "Thank you, Freddy."

"We'll be leaving soon," Hunt said. "Would you like to see how we do it?"

"I would indeed."

Hunt took the doctor up to the control deck and strapped him onto an acceleration couch facing the astrogation sphere. "Prepare for departure, Freddy," Hunt ordered.

"Aye, sir," Freddy said.

The clamps on the far end of the snake opened with their familiar metallic bumps and grinds, and the astrogation sphere showed Hunt the course back to Earth that Freddy had plotted. Jan reported in ready.

"Ready here, Raymond," Freddy said.

"Let's go," Hunt said.

A green dot appeared near the center of the sphere, and the main thrusters flung the *Heinlein* on its way.

* * * *

Hunt wanted to study, but he had a distinguished passenger now, so he also had an obligation to be entertaining. Hunt's life was made easier because the doctor had spent so much of his time alone that it did not bother him. He read a lot and watched some of the new holos they'd brought with them. But the doctor didn't spend all his time by himself. Hunt learned that the doctor was a demon checkers player—he enjoyed it as a blood sport.

Hunt, Eignbergen, and Jan were sitting in the tiny galley eating *sparkzel*, one of Jan's Venusian specialties; it was a lumpy mix of vegetables that grew all over Venus since the terraforming, and seasoned with swamp mist— when Jan brought up the question that Hunt was too polite to ask. "So, Doctor, what exactly have you been working on for ten years?"

"Now, Jan," Hunt said, "It's possible that Doctor E would rather not say."

For a long moment Eignbergen contemplated the intent and serious expression on Jan's face while taking another forkful of *sparkzel*, a dish that he seemed to like. "I don't want to bore you," he said.

"That's nice of you," Jan said. "But hanging out with Hunt here, I have a high tolerance for that sort of thing."

Both Hunt and Eignbergen laughed at that. The expression on Jan's face didn't change.

"All right, then. If you insist." The doctor carefully set down his fork and asked Hunt to guide them to the storage bay. When they arrived, they approached the big box in the middle of the deck. Jan watched Eignbergen expectantly.

Eignbergen shook his head. "Poor Covington," he said sadly, as if he were talking to himself.

"Who's Covington?" Hunt couldn't help asking.

Eignbergen looked at Hunt suddenly, as if he'd forgotten he wasn't alone. The doctor sighed. "Albert Covington. He volunteered to be the first to try the machine. He never came back."

"What sort of machine is it?" Jan asked.

"Oh, didn't I tell you? It's a time machine."

"You gotta be—" Jan began.

"You mean this fellow Covington is lost somewhere in time?" Hunt asked, heading Jan off before he said something they would all regret.

Eignbergen nodded.

"Past or future?" Jan asked.

"I'm not sure," Dr. Eignbergen said. "Past, I think. Here, I'll show you." He walked to the big case and undid the clasps. The box unfolded to reveal a complex collection of long thin silver rods seemingly stuck at random into a glowing sphere in the center of a cubical frame; it was very much like the astrogation sphere in the control room of the *RAH* but much smaller. Hunt had trouble following some of the rods with his eyes—they went off in some indefinable direction and didn't seem quite real.

"What are those rods made of?" Hunt asked.

"A little something of my own," Dr. Eignbergen said. "I call it temporine. The rods manipulate the tachyons."

"Temporal, as in time," Jan guessed.

"Exactly. And tachyon is a term coined by Gerald Feinberg back in 1967, but he had no idea what to do with the word because he hadn't actually found the particle it described—neither had anybody else, until I had a thought. Ten years ago all I wanted to do was find a new method of preserving food. You'd put food into the box I wanted to invent, and when you took it out years later it would still be fresh because only seconds had passed inside."

"Sounds like a good idea," Hunt said.

"It was. It still is. I hoped to finish the invention before the grant money ran out and I had to go back to Earth. And I might have succeeded, I suppose. Only the longer I worked, the further I got from food preservation and the more involved I became with time travel. After a while I dropped the food preservation idea altogether. This is the result." He nodded at the thing that had been inside the case.

"Does it work? Jan asked.

Eignbergen made a "harrumphing" noise. "Ask Albert Covington," he said.

They all considered that for a moment.

"Would you like to see it in action?" Eignbergen asked.

"I believe we would, yes," Hunt said.

Eignbergen twisted rods at the corners of the array, causing indicators to appear floating over the top of the box, and lights began to move inside the sphere. The doctor sucked on his lower lip as he made further adjustments with the rods while watching the numbers registering on his gauges. "There we are," he said. "A *Space League* episode broadcast live in 1955 to television sets all over what was then the United States."

And sure enough, the lights inside the sphere settled down into a black and white image. Two men in fancy uniforms—each a cross between a holo adventure cowboy outfit and something an actor playing Robin Hood might wear—stood near a wooden desk studying a box with a flashing bulb on top and a lot of knobs on the sides. "Looks kind of old-fashioned," Jan said scornfully.

"That shouldn't surprise you," Dr. Eignbergen explained. "In addition to their tiny budget, *Space League* was produced a few hundred years in our past."

"I'm impressed," Hunt said. "Considering. Can you turn up the gain on the sound?"

Dr. Eignbergen twisted one of the rods.

"Is that how the Amethyst Queen has been making her ship invisible, Commodore Edwards?" asked the younger of the two men in the sphere.

"I believe so, Cadet Jolly."

The two looked surprised when a beautiful woman marched into the room. She wore a long silvery cloak, a complicated headdress, and a lot of eye makeup, making her appear as if she were looking out through a mask made from the wings of a Terran butterfly.

"The Amethyst Queen!" Jolly exclaimed. "How did you get in here?"

"It is not difficult when you can make yourself invisible," she said and smiled sweetly.

"What do you want?" the older man demanded.

"You know the answer to that," the Amethyst Queen said. "I want the destruction of the Space League Academy."

The two uniformed men shared a horrified look.

The picture faded, and for a moment Hunt thought that something had gone wrong with the doctor's machine. But the scene they'd been watching was immediately replaced by a different man in a different place in a similar uniform. Before him on a table was a tall rectangular box and a large bowl.

"Hey, kids," the man said enthusiastically, "you still have time to get your *Space League* decoder badge from Sugar Slammers, the spaceman's breakfast." He went on and on about all the wonderful things the badge could do, and how great Sugar Slammers were for breakfast. "Good and good for ya!"

"This is what they thought you System Guard cadets would be like," the doctor said, and chuckled.

"Ridiculous," Jan said.

"Not a bad guess from hundreds of years in the past," Hunt said. "Good-looking uniforms."

Jan sniffed at that.

"And after all," the doctor said, "the show was entertainment, not a documentary."

An alert chirped three times, and Freddy came on the air. "Raymond, we are receiving a message from a small ship five thousand klicks off our starboard bow," he reported calmly.

"Let's hear it," Hunt said.

"Mayday, Mayday, this is *Forty-Niner* calling anyone."

"It sounds like a woman," Jan noted.

She repeated her message.

"This is the System Guard scout ship *Robert A. Heinlein*," Hunt said. "What is your situation?"

"Thank Frooth," the woman said. "I've been struck by a meteor, and the puncture is too big for my emergency system to handle. Not much air left." And indeed, she did sound a little out of breath.

"Freddy, make course for *Forty-Niner*," Hunt ordered.

CHAPTER 3

TIME FOR MS. GARLEY

The *Forty-Niner* was considerably smaller than the *Heinlein*. It looked something like a gray pumpkin, a design that had been old decades before. With Freddy's help, *Heinlein* came alongside and matched velocities. Hunt adjusted the *Heinlein's* airlock until it fit snugly against the one on the *Forty-Niner*.

"Anybody else?" Hunt asked as a woman climbed through the lock and boarded the scout ship.

"Nope," she said. "Just li'l ol' me." She was a small woman wearing a baggy, olive-drab outfit. Short dark hair hung every which-way around her head and in front of her pretty face. She'd been banged up pretty badly.

Hunt introduced everyone, and Dr. Eignbergen gravely shook her hand.

"I'm Bernadette Garley," she said.

"Dangerous being all alone out here," Hunt said.

"I've been prospecting," she told them, and took a deep breath. "I guess the System Guard is good for something after all."

"Excuse me?" Jan exclaimed. Hunt just looked at her with amazement.

"Most of the time you boys are so busy saluting each other I'm surprised you heard my distress call."

"That's not exactly—" Hunt began.

She interrupted him. "No need to explain," she said. "My brother was in the Guard. He was killed in the Second Jovian Campaign."

"I'm sorry," Hunt said.

"His commanding officer was an idiot," Garley stated firmly.

Hunt knew that sort of thing happened occasionally, but not very often. He let her accusation stand. "If you'd like," he said, "I'll show you to my cabin. I'll sleep on one of the acceleration couches on the control deck."

"Thanks," Garley said, as if she'd expected Hunt to make just that sort of dumb offer.

"Freddy, attach an astrogation beacon to Ms. Garley's ship. She can figure out what to do with it later."

"Aye, Raymond."

* * * *

Dr. Eignbergen closed up the case containing the time machine and strolled away, probably back to his cabin, Hunt thought. During the afternoon, Jan watched over the power deck, and Hunt went up to the control deck where he studied the sphere for his stellar astrogation class.

He'd been at it only a few minutes when Garley rose through the drop shaft and stepped off onto the control deck. She glanced around for a moment as if she hoped to find something she'd lost. Hunt tried to ignore her as she wandered around the deck, trailing her fingers across the bulkheads, studying the controls and instruments.

Shortly, Hunt could stand the intrusion no longer. "Can I help you with something?" he asked, hoping she would tell him he couldn't, and then retreat.

"No. I'm just kind of interested in ships."

"Let me know if you have any questions," Hunt said, and returned to his work.

She didn't have any questions, but she didn't go away either. "Freddy," Hunt said, "would you please ask Cadet Jan to come up here?"

"Of course, Raymond."

Jan arrived a few minutes later, looking slightly irritated. "I hope this is important," he said.

"Jan," Hunt said, "Ms. Garley is interested in ships. Would you please give her a tour of the *Heinlein*?"

Jan grinned. "Delighted," he said. "Right this way, Ms. Garley."

At first she looked as annoyed as Jan had, but then something changed her mind, and she took Jan's arm. "Lead the way, Cadet Jan," she said merrily.

Hunt watched them go while he contemplated Garley's sudden change of manner. The little he knew about her did not inspire trust. Still, Jan was no fool. Not much could go wrong if he was with her.

Hunt went back to his studying, and was so deeply involved in it that when Freddy spoke to him, the voice startled him as if from a sound sleep. "What is it, Freddy?"

"Cadet Jan told Ms. Garley about Dr. Eignbergen's time machine, and she asked to see it. They are on their way to the storage bay."

Hunt wasn't sure if that was important, but even so, the thought of Garley trailing her fingers through a machine that had caused Albert Covington to be lost in time gave him an uneasy feeling.

"On my way," he said as he got up from his acceleration couch.

When Hunt entered the storage bay he saw that at the other end of the big room the bay's auxiliary door was sliding closed slowly with a grate and a grunt. Jan already had the doctor's case open. With intense concentration, he and Garley were looking at the time machine.

"Can you make it work?" Garley asked.

"Of course," Jan said, though Hunt knew it wasn't true. Jan understood as little about the machine as he did. Jan held his hands over the rods, not quite sure where to put them down, then chose one—arbitrarily, Hunt thought—and twisted it. The video sphere appeared in the center of the array.

"What are you doing, Cadet Jan?" Hunt asked.

Jan looked up with surprise. "Hi there, Hunt," Jan said in his usual overly confident way. "Just showing Ms. Garley the ship like you asked me to."

Inside the sphere, the same scene they had already seen before played out again. Once again Cadet Jolly and Commodore Edwards discussed the Amethyst Queen's ability to make her ships invisible, and once again the two were surprised to see the Amethyst Queen herself enter the room.

"I like her," Garley said after a moment. "She knows what she wants and she doesn't take guff from anybody."

The scene faded out, and the commercial for Sugar Slammers began.

"I think that's enough," Hunt said, and strode forward, intending to close up the case. But before he could do so, Garley grabbed another one of the rods. "I wonder what this one does," she said as she twisted it.

"Don't!" Hunt cried.

But the sphere at the center of the machine had already grown into a pale blue bubble, and for just a second Hunt saw all three of them reflected in its smooth surface. It quickly grew large enough to envelope the machine and then continued to grow until it completely enclosed them too.

The bubble exploded like an over-inflated balloon and suddenly they were no longer aboard the *Heinlein*.

CHAPTER 4

CLASSY UNIFORMS

"That was a crazy thing to do, Ms. Garley," Hunt said as he struggled to sit up.

"Who knew it would actually work?" Garley asked with innocent surprise.

"Where are we?" Jan asked. He was sitting up by now, but appeared just as confused as the other two. The doctor's time machine still stood nearby, as it had been before the explosion.

Jan's question was a good one. They had landed—if that was the word—on a cement floor between a wall covered with thick yellow spongy stuff and a wall that seemed little more than a thin sheet supported by a wooden framework. From the high ceiling hung banks of bright lights. Muffled voices came from the other side of the thin sheet. Hunt was surprised that he recognized them.

"Is that how the Amethyst Queen has been making her ship invisible, Commodore Edwards?" asked one of the voices.

"I believe so, Cadet Jolly," the other answered.

"It's the scene Dr. Eignbergen showed us," Jan said with amazement. "They must be running it again."

"We're dealing with a time machine, Jan," Hunt said. "Maybe if they're running again, it's for the first and only time."

"Huh?"

"Think it over. Using our time machine we can travel over the same moment as often as we like."

Jan nodded.

"And if Dr. Eignbergen is right about when they produced this show," Hunt continued, "we must be back in the 1950s."

"Isn't that when Andrew Gordon started his flying school?" Jan asked.

"Who's Andrew Gordon?" Garley asked. She was watching them with amusement while lying on her side, supporting herself on one elbow.

"A few years from now, his flying school will become the System Guard Academy," Hunt explained.

"Really?" Garley remarked as if this amazing fact impressed her. After that she got quiet and thoughtful.

"There must be a way to find Andrew Gordon in this primitive era," Jan suggested.

"Why find him?" Hunt asked.

"Just to say 'hi.' He'd probably be glad to see us."

"Maybe." Hunt was doubtful.

A couple of big, casually-dressed men hurried around one side of the thin sheet of wall, each with a finger to his lips, shushing them.

Jan opened his mouth to say something, but he stopped when one of the big men glared at him. On the other side of the wall the *Space League* episode continued. The commercial for Sugar Slammers stressing the absolute necessity of having a *Space League* decoder badge, ran to its inevitable conclusion, followed by some march music. A loud bell rang once, filling the big room with sound.

"What are you yoyos doing back here?" one of the big men asked.

Apparently it was all right to talk now. "I'm afraid we're a little lost," Hunt said.

"That's for sure," the other big man said. "And I've never seen uniforms like those before. You better come with us to see Mr. Thrash."

The big men escorted Hunt, Jan, and Garley around the end of the thin sheet and the three found themselves in the room with the switch box, supposedly the gadget that made the Amethyst Queen's ships invisible, resting on the desk. The light bulb on top was no longer flashing.

The Commodore's office had no fourth wall, but opened onto a space much bigger than the office itself. It was filled with scattered folding chairs and equipment Hunt had seen only in photographs and documentaries about the good old days. The area could have accommodated a large audience, but the activity and the equipment in it told Hunt that the fellows there were working and not waiting to be entertained. Some men were sweeping with big push brooms, and others were moving equipment and furniture—controlled chaos. There were big metal boxes from which thick black cables wound to other big metal boxes. Members of the crew were very busy unplugging the cables and winding them into tight professional coils. Alien-looking apparatuses that might have been cameras were large and bulky, lenses projecting from their fronts like noses. Despite the size of the cameras, the technicians moved each of them easily on a thick column rolling on a wide wheeled base.

The two big men guided Hunt and the others to a chubby man wearing a brown sweater and a bow tie with matching polka-dots. Glasses rested on a fleshy nose, and what was left of his white hair was so fine that it looked like mist rising from the top of his head. He was talking to a young woman wearing practical shoes and a dark blue outfit. She took quick notes on paper held against a clipboard, then ran off like the White Rabbit, late for an appointment.

"Al, have you seen Mr. Thrash?" one of the big men asked the man in the polka-dot bow tie.

"He was here a minute ago," Al said. He stared at Hunt and Jan and smiled with appreciation. "Nice uniforms," he said.

"Thanks," Jan said, as if he was not sure how to take Al's compliment.

Hunt introduced himself, Jan, and Garley.

"We found them behind the Commodore's office set. We don't know how they got there or what they had in mind."

"I'll handle this, Charlie," the chubby man said.

Charlie hesitated for a moment.

"Go home, Charlie," Al said. It was more of an order than a suggestion.

Al continued to study the three after Charlie and his friend hurried off. "What *were* you doing back there?" Al asked.

For a moment Hunt was prepared to tell the truth, but he didn't see any percentage in that. If Al believed him— unlikely at best—the three time-travelers would suddenly become the center of an unpleasant uproar. More questions were sure to follow. If Al didn't believe him, they would all have a good laugh, and Hunt would just have to come up with another, more believable, story.

"We're tourists," Jan said off-handedly. "You know, just looking around."

"What do *you* do here?" Garley asked, giving Al a big smile.

"I write most of the *Space League* episodes."

"You must be very creative," Garley said, "to speculate on what the future is going to be like."

"I do my best. The thing about my job I like most is that nobody around here can say that I'm wrong." He rubbed his chin. "Except maybe you guys. Like I said, nice uniforms."

Hunt didn't know quite what to make of Al's last remark. "What would we know about the future?" he asked.

Al smiled at that, but said nothing.

"We're big *Space League* fans," Jan said. "We had the uniforms made up special." Hunt looked at Jan with admiration. It was as good an explanation as any, but Hunt was still suspicious. He looked forward to a time when he could question Al alone.

"Tell me all about the Amethyst Queen," Garley said, and put her arm through Al's. Al seemed surprised by this, but he didn't pull away.

Hunt had no idea what Garley might have in mind, but he was sure that it was something he would not like.

Cadet Jolly and Commodore Edwards approached them across the large empty floor, each wearing a coat and tie. They looked odd out of uniform.

"Good show," the Commodore said.

"Thanks, Bill," Al said. "You fellows always make me look good."

"See you tomorrow," Jolly said.

The Commodore looked at the visitors. "What are you fellows made up for?" he asked.

"We're fans of the show," Hunt said. "This is just a design of our own. Do you like it?"

"I wish we could get uniforms that grand," the Commodore said as he felt the material in Hunt's shirt cuff. "Say, what is this stuff anyway? It feels like paper, and then it doesn't." He frowned.

"I don't know," Hunt said, trying to sound sincere. "We bought a few yards of it back home."

"Grand."

"Talk to Thrash," Al suggested. "Maybe he'll get you some."

Jolly and the Commodore laughed as they strolled off in opposite directions.

"You were going to tell me about the Amethyst Queen," Garley said.

"I was," Al said, "but now I don't have to. She can tell you about herself."

Like the rest of the people attached to the show, the two walking toward them were casually dressed. Nevertheless, Hunt could see that their clothing was expensive—nicely designed, beautifully cut—for this era, anyway. The man was all in brown—apparently this year's color—with a jacket that was a few shades lighter. He was handsome enough to be an actor himself, with a square chin and iron-gray eyes. A couple of points of black hair fell against one of his eyebrows.

The woman wore a tight black skirt that barely allowed her to take a step, and a blouse with a big bow that was pale pink, like the inside of a seashell. Her shoes were blocky and had very high heels. Though she wasn't wearing her butterfly makeup, Hunt could tell that she was the woman who played the Amethyst Queen. Garley knew it too. Her eyes got wide. She straightened and smiled, showing her teeth.

"What have we here?" the man asked.

"Fans of the show," Al said.

"Nice uniforms," the man said. "We should do something like that."

"Boys and girls, this is Mr. Christopher Thrash, the producer of *Space League*."

Mr. Thrash shook hands all around, paying particular attention to Garley. The woman with him waited patiently, an expression of studied disinterest on her face. Apparently, she had seen him shake hands before and was neither impressed nor amused.

"This is our villainess," Al said, "The Amethyst Queen—known to her friends as Eunice Quigley."

Garley unwrapped herself from around Al, and approached her. "I want to hear all about your plan to destroy the *Space League* Academy," she said with bright curiosity.

"Huh?" Eunice Quigley asked, looking baffled.

"Eunice, you go with Al," Mr. Thrash said. "I'll take care of Miss Garley."

"I'll bet," Eunice Quigley said.

Thrash ignored her remark and strolled off with Garley.

"Wait a minute," Hunt called after her. He didn't know how long he and Jan would remain in the 1950s, and he didn't want to leave Garley behind when they went home. Suddenly, worry struck him like lightning. Was the time machine still where they'd left it? Was it safe anywhere? Hunt got the feeling that they should be leaving.

"Let her go," Jan said. "You're not responsible for her."

"No, but still—"

"But still, we're ignoring Al and Miss Quigley."

It was true. He and Jan were being rude. And if Garley was left behind it was obviously nobody's fault but her own. Even so, Hunt felt guilty for allowing her to walk off like that. As for the time machine, there seemed to be a lot of expensive equipment and futuristic gadgets around here. Anybody who came by would probably assume the time machine was just one more prop. Curious about this time period, he decided to let it all go—for the moment, anyway.

"You hungry, Eunice?" Al asked. "What about you guys?"

Everybody was, and Al offered to take them to a restaurant he knew. He walked them out of the big building into the late afternoon sunshine, where they cast long shadows as black as space. They walked down a paved street between enormous buildings much like the one they'd come out of, ignored by men pushing big lights on standards, and by women, many of whom were dressed mostly in glitter and feathers. What was another futuristic uniform more or less?

Al showed them out to a big paved field where a lot of smooth metal machines were hunched together in rows. Hunt thought they might be what were called automobiles. He'd seen an example in a museum once, though these were even more ancient than the one he'd seen. Al opened a door in the side of a yellow automobile, pulled forward the padded backrest of one side of the front couch, and invited Hunt and Jan to climb into the back, where there was another couch, as wide as the automobile, upholstered in some soft gray material. He let the backrest fall back into place, and helped Eunice Quigley into the right side of the front couch. Hunt and Jan jumped when he swung the door closed with a loud bang. Then he ran around to the other side of the automobile and got in under a big, nearly vertical wheel. He made another loud bang with his door. Hunt and Jan watched with interest as he turned a key in a slot in the control board before him, and a motor roared to life.

"Yow!" Jan cried.

Hunt gripped a padded shelf in the door on his side. He'd never heard anything like that sound. But the adventure was only beginning. Al adjusted a lever alongside the big wheel, and the automobile backed up. He moved the lever again and the automobile rolled forward slowly through the field along an aisle between parked automobiles. Soon they were out on the street, where Al speeded up considerably. Everything around Hunt was a blur: buildings, people, other automobiles. They were rolling along too quickly for him to see any details.

"I don't feel so good," Jan said.

Hunt felt a little woozy himself. "Where are you taking us?" he asked.

"Little place I know," Al said. "The Shanghai Café. It's kind of a Hollywood landmark."

"Is it far?" Jan asked. He was clutching the padded shelf on his side of the car, and he did not look happy.

"Ten, fifteen minutes depending on traffic," Al said. The automobile stopped to allow other automobiles to cross in front of them. He glanced into the back seat. "You fellows okay?" he asked, a big grin on his face.

"Fine," Hunt said unconvincingly, and swallowed hard. He closed his eyes and concentrated on keeping breakfast down. Neither Al nor Eunice Quigley seemed to be in any distress, so apparently people could get used to traveling this way. Adapting could not happen too soon for him.

CHAPTER 5

STUPID OR JUST NAÏVE?

At last Al turned into another parking field and found an empty place among the few stationary automobiles. He turned off the motor, got out, and walked around to the other side of his automobile, where he helped Eunice out.

Hunt and Jan hadn't moved. Now that the automobile had stopped, Hunt felt a little better, but he continued to vibrate as if the automobile were still moving. He certainly didn't feel like eating. He wasn't even sure he could stand up just yet.

"You fellows coming?" Al yelled in through the open door. He pulled the front couch backrest forward.

Moving carefully, balancing every part of his body just so, Hunt got out of the automobile followed by Jan, who also seemed to be moving with unnatural care. The two cadets followed Eunice Quigley and Al across the paved field to a long low building that seemed to be padded on the outside with dense red fabric. A wooden sign down the length of the building said SHANGHAI CAFÉ. They pushed through a heavy wooden door painted with characters Hunt had never seen before, and into a dim room lit by occasional red electric lanterns. A bar extended down the length of the room and across from it, taking up one whole wall, was a line of booths padded in the same red stuff. Three men were at the bar talking about something called "baseball," and in one of the booths a glum man and woman sat ignoring each other while they drank and smoked.

"Hi, Al," the bartender called.

"Hi, Seymour," Al called back. He ushered them to one of the empty booths, and Seymour came by with four cardboard cards, each a little bigger than a hand. "I don't suppose either of you birds has any money," Al said.

Hunt hadn't been carrying any money on the *Heinlein*, of course, and it hadn't occurred to him until this moment that they would need some sort of physical exchange to make purchases here. Commerce was different at home.

Jan laughed uneasily. "Isn't our credit good?" he asked, causing the others to stare at him in wonder.

"Take it easy, Jan," Hunt said. "Uh, no we don't," he continued to Al.

"That's okay," Al said. "You'll owe me." He smiled at Eunice Quigley. "What'll you have?" he asked.

Hunt studied his card, which turned out to be a menu. Though the menu was printed in English characters, many of the words themselves might as well have been in Old High Venusian. From the confused expression on Jan's face, he was having the same problem.

"What would you suggest?" Hunt asked.

"The Chinese food is pretty good, but I think Eunice and I are going to have hamburgers. It's been a specialty of the house since Buster Keaton used to eat here with his director thirty years ago."

Hunt had no idea who Buster Keaton was, or why he would need someone to direct him.

"Sounds good," Jan said, and Hunt agreed.

Seymour came over with a pad and pencil. Al ordered, and included some French fries, whatever they were, for the table.

"Sure thing, boss," Seymour said as he hurried away.

"We enjoyed your performance as the Amethyst Queen," Jan said.

"Thanks," Eunice Quigley said, taking the compliment without even a smile. She lit a cigarette, and Hunt tried without much luck to avoid the smoke.

"Where are you fellows from?" Al asked.

"Around," Hunt said. "Not far from here, actually."

"Ah," Al said as if he'd expected just that.

"Tell us about Christopher Thrash," Hunt suggested, hoping to change the subject.

"As I said, he's the producer of *Space League*. He also owns a big chunk of the company that makes Sugar Slammers."

"That figures," Jan remarked. "I guess he'll be able to tell Ms. Garley everything she wants to know about destroying the Academy."

"Everything that I've written so far," Al admitted.

"That's more than I know," Eunice said. "The only script I've seen is tomorrow's. But by this time Chris and your Miss Garley have probably gone way beyond that."

"What do you mean?" Hunt asked.

Eunice looked at him with surprise. "Are you stupid or just naïve?" she remarked.

"Your choice," Jan said as he laughed.

Seymour came back carrying a tray with four sweating brown glass bottles and set one down in front of each of them. He also had a bowl full of long thin sticks that he placed in the middle of the table. The sticks were a light yellow with browner areas that make them look as if they'd been baked or deep-fried or something. They smelled wonderful, making Hunt realize how hungry he was—which was a relief after the wooziness he'd felt in the automobile.

"French fries," Al said as Seymour set down a tall thin bottle full of red stuff next to them.

Al had trouble starting the thick red sludge in the bottle, but at last a lot of it poured out at once. He didn't seem upset as the goo ran all over the French fries. Hunt and Jan just stared at the resulting mess.

Eunice began to pull fries out through the red stuff, then stopped suddenly. "What's wrong?" she asked.

"Don't be bashful, gentlemen," Al said. "Enough for all."

Thinking that he'd be happier with some of Jan's Venusian food, Hunt experimentally pulled a French fry from the bowl; he could not help smiling when he began to chew. "Amazing," he said. "Are these things really from France?" he asked.

"Good question," was the only answer Al gave them.

Jan took one of the French fries and responded as Hunt had. "What is this red stuff?" he asked.

"Ketchup," Al replied. "Don't you have ketchup where you come from?"

"Oh, sure," Jan said airily. "Ours is just a different shade of red."

"I'll bet," Al said.

While they continued to scarf up French fries, Seymour returned carrying four plates with the ease of a professional. In the center of each plate was a small round loaf of bread sliced in half horizontally. Layered between the two halves was food that Hunt could not immediately identify.

"Meat, onions, lettuce, tomatoes," Al explained.

"Sure," Jan said. "We have that on Venus."

"Where?" Eunice exclaimed.

"That's the street he lives on," Hunt explained.

"Home sweet home," Jan said, and took a big bite of his hamburger.

The four of them worked on their hamburgers for a few minutes, stopping only to sip beer or chomp on more French fries. The hamburger grease and the ketchup ran down their fingers. Hunt found that the paper napkins Seymour brought were very useful.

Now that his hunger was blunted, Hunt began to think about Garley again. "Where do you think Mr. Thrash took Ms. Garley?" he asked.

They all looked at Eunice Quigley. She calmly sipped from her brown bottle. "Could be a few places," she said at last. "If he didn't immediately take her to his mansion in Beverly Hills, he might have taken her downtown to impress her with Stormfield Storage, where he keeps all the expensive furniture and paintings that don't fit into his house. At least that's where he took me. He rotates stuff in and out every few months."

"You don't sound jealous," Jan commented.

"No point," Eunice said. "Any girl who believes she can tie Chris down is kidding herself. Good luck to your friend is what I say. Besides, he'll come back to me when you three go home—wherever that is."

When he finished his meal Hunt felt full, but pleasantly so. He would miss the cooking in this era when he got home—if he got home. Garley could stay here if she wanted to, but he and Jan had to find the time machine and get back to the *Heinlein*. He wondered how much time would have passed. Would Eignbergen still be napping? Would years have passed or only seconds? All this ran through his mind while the four of them sat digesting and rubbing their fingers with paper napkins to get the ketchup and grease off.

"Why is Miss Garley so interested in what the Amethyst Queen wants to do with the *Space League* Academy?" Eunice asked.

Jan looked at Hunt. Hunt thought about Garley's problem with the System Guard.

"She's just a fan like we are," Hunt said.

"I believe you, though thousands might not," Eunice said.

Al paid the bill, and drove them back to the studio. Hunt didn't feel so queasy on the ride back, though he was full of food. Perhaps he was getting used to riding in an automobile—certainly a useful skill in this day and age.

"Where to, boys?" Al asked as he pulled into the nearly empty lot. Eunice turned and with mild curiosity, stared at them over the back of the seat.

It was a good question. The answer depended a lot on how much they could trust Al. So far he seemed like a valuable man to know, but despite the fact he'd bought them a meal, that wasn't really a reliable hook from which to hang trust. At first Hunt considered asking him to take them to Christopher Thrash's Beverly Hills home—wherever Beverly Hills was—to see if they could convince Garley to join them. Which was a good idea if she wasn't so hostile that she'd get in their way. They might do better finding the time machine on their own. They could pick up Garley later if she was willing.

"Oh, just anywhere," Hunt said casually, hoping that he and Jan could find the time machine without Al's help.

"You sure?" Al asked.

"We're sure," Jan said with more certainty than Hunt felt.

Al slowed his automobile to a stop and looked back at them worriedly, as if he was sure he was letting them out into the trackless wilderness.

"Okay," he said. Without turning off the engine, he got out of the automobile, opened the door, and pulled the backrest forward. Eunice wished Jan and Hunt a good evening as they got out. They waved as Al drove across the field and out into the street. A moment later Al's car, taking Eunice and Al with it, was lost in the traffic.

Hunt wondered why Al was being so helpful, all without asking any of the questions one might reasonably ask a couple of uniformed boys such as Jan and himself.

CHAPTER 6

ESCAPE ABOARD THE *MAGELLAN*

They set off for the location where they'd first appeared. The sun had nearly set, and big harsh lights aimed from rooftops shown down on them, illuminating their progress. After losing their way a few times, they arrived at the big square building they were looking for. Jan yanked on the door handle. It was locked of course.

"Now what?" Jan asked. "Can we break in?"

Hunt glared at the heavy door as if it had personally offended him. "Before we do that, let's make sure that we have to." Hunt began moving a finger in a pattern on the opposite cuff of his uniform shirt.

Jan grinned. "The percepticon, of course," he said. He watched over Hunt's shoulder as his cuff began to glow. "Tachyons," Jan stated.

"Yeah," Hunt agreed. Only the time machine would give them off. Nobody in this era had even heard of them. "Now we break in."

But before they had a chance to do more than talk about their plan, they were stopped by a loud voice. "Hey! You there! What are you doing?"

A thin man wearing glasses and a contemporary uniform had obviously just come around a corner while pulling a weapon from a holster at his hip.

Hunt and Jan didn't wait to find out if they could convince the guard that they were part of the *Space League* crew. They ran. Quick footsteps hurried after them and grew closer. The guard was pretty fast for an old guy. A single gunshot echoed off the blank wall of the big building they wanted to get into.

Hunt and Jan ran faster, and were soon lost in a wild jungle of cables, electronic equipment, furniture, painted backgrounds, and big trucks. They could hear the guard walking nearby, hidden by a wall of fake ivy. The footsteps stopped. Hunt and Jan waited without moving, almost without breathing. The footsteps moved on. Hunt tapped Jan on the shoulder and pointed, indicating that they should also move along.

They came to a wide driveway where a long motorized vehicle was parked—obviously designed to carry freight of some kind. Hunt was astonished to see that loaded on the flatbed of the vehicle was a structure unlike anything they might have expected in this year or even this century—a dart-shaped ship very much like *Heinlein* but resting on skids. Written on the nose of the ship in letters that resembled lightning bolts was the word *Magellan*.

They approached the *Magellan* slowly, as if something might jump out at them from the darkness inside the open hatch. They heard footsteps—certainly the guard coming back this way—and hurried across the pavement to the ship. They crouched in the darkness just inside the hatch and waited for the guard to pass. They saw him glance this way and that, but he kept walking.

"That was close," Jan remarked softly.

Hunt did not respond, but looked around, allowing his eyes to adjust. Dim light reflecting off the wall of a nearby building entered the ship through the big cat's eye ports at the bow and lit the interior. Controls and instruments covered the walls, except in a recess where a pair of bunk beds were stacked. Two acceleration couches faced the main control panel under the front ports.

Hunt reached out through the open doorway and felt for the hatch, which was open against the hull of the ship. When he pulled the hatch closed he was surprised to learn how light it was. He guessed it was made of wood. And it did not thump convincingly against the hull of the ship like an automobile door, but made a gentle click.

"It's not an airlock," Jan said. "It's just a door."

"And this may not be a real ship," Hunt suggested. He marched up the center of the ship and sat down in one of the couches. He gingerly touched the controls; some were made of wood and others of metal, but they all moved easily up and down or around as if not connected to anything. The instruments were also useless—they were painted onto the control board.

"Well?" Jan asked as he looked over Hunt's shoulder.

"All fake," Hunt said.

"You think it has something to do with the television show?"

"Good guess."

"Look," Jan said, "I'm sorry about all this."

"About all what?" Hunt said, although he knew.

"I guess we're in kind of a bad spot here."

"We will be if we don't find that time machine."

"I was just trying to impress Garley. I thought maybe showing her the time machine might prove to her that we System Guards aren't so bad. I didn't know she was going to mess with it."

"Look, Longwood," Hunt said, "none of that matters now—though I admit it would have been smarter of you not to give her a tour that was quite so complete."

Longwood Jan nodded sadly.

"As far as proving that System Guards aren't so bad, you'll recall that by the time Ms. Garley requested a tour we'd already saved her life."

Jan nodded again. Hunt could see he was having a very bad day.

Hunt opened the doorway slightly, and peered out at the studio. "Let's go," he said.

"Go where?" Jan asked.

"The time machine?" Hunt reminded him.

"Personally, I could use a nap."

"Personally," Hunt replied, "I would rather find that time machine before somebody else gets hold of it."

Jan nodded with weary understanding, then pushed past him. Hunt followed him back to the locked door that had the time machine behind it. They contemplated the door for a moment, then Hunt made a pattern on his cuff that would aim the weapon that was part of his uniform.

But before Hunt had a chance to blast the lock open, two guards came around the corner—the old gentleman who had chased them into the *Magellan*, and a much younger, more energetic companion. Hunt did not like the look of the spring in the younger guard's step. He and Jan backed into the thick darkness, then set off at a run. The old guard stayed at the door, while the younger one followed Hunt and Jan.

Hunt and Jan got lost among the big square buildings, the fake brick walls, the forests of lights, and hulking automobiles lined up, nose to tail, like domesticated animals. They stopped now and again to listen for the footsteps of the young guard. They waited while the foot-steps seemed to get farther away, then moved on.

Worn out and sweaty, Hunt and Jan accidentally came upon the *Magellan* again.

"I'm convinced," Hunt said when they were safely inside. "Morning is soon enough to find the machine. We can arrive with the rest of the *Space League* crew. You want the top bunk or the bottom?"

Jan chose the top bunk, which was sort of an admission of how guilty he felt, because Hunt knew he'd favored bottom bunks since joining the service.

Hunt lay down on the bottom bunk and tried to get comfortable. Above him, Jan continued to move around, flopping this way and that. It would be a long night.

"Ray?"

"What?" Hunt asked, trying not to sound as irritated as he felt. He'd been right on the edge of sleep.

"Why do you think Garley is so interested in the Amethyst Queen's plan to destroy the *Space League* Academy?"

"Why do *you* think?" Hunt shot right back. He wasn't about to do Jan's surmising for him.

There was a long silence. "I think she wants to destroy the real System Guard Academy," Jan said, "and she thinks that the Amethyst Queen might have a terrific idea about how to do it." Jan suddenly laughed.

"What?" Hunt asked, mystified by his sudden delight.

"Whatever Garley decided to do, she obviously failed."

"How do you figure?"

"If she somehow succeeded stopping the establishment of the Academy here in the past, we would never have gone to the Academy ourselves because there wouldn't have been one."

Hunt considered Jan's argument. It sounded good but there was something wrong with it. He stared into the darkness trying to decide where the defect was. "Longwood?" Hunt said at last.

"Yes?"

"Your argument would be just fine if we were dealing with a linear universe. But we know very little about time travel, and what it does to cause and effect. And even less about whether we came from the same universe as the one we are in now, or if we are dealing with an infinite number of parallel universes, each just a little different from all the others. In how many of them did Garley succeed? If and when we return to our own time, will we find that things are the same, or that they have been changed by what we do here and now?"

A heavy sigh came from above. "You think too much, Ray," Jan said. He turned over one more time and then all was still. Hunt counted Jan's snores as he drifted off to sleep.

* * * *

Hunt was shaken awake by the sudden movement of his bunk.

"Whoa!" Jan cried.

For a moment Hunt forgot where he was and why, but when he opened his eyes and saw the interior of the fake ship around him, he remembered everything.

The ship rocked a little and vibrated as if it were moving, and somewhere nearby a big motor growled—the great-grandfather of the motor that powered Al's automobile.

Missing the Sleep-Away he usually woke to, Hunt rolled out of the bunk and rubbed his face as he stepped carefully up the center aisle to the front of the ship. Out the front ports he saw that the flatbed on which the ship rested was attached to some kind of machine that was pulling it down the driveway and through the studio, barely getting by without a scrape in some of the narrowest places.

"Where are we going?" Jan asked.

"No idea," Hunt said. "But we're on our way."

The machine pulled the flatbed out into the street and merged with the early morning traffic. To begin with there wasn't much of it, but soon automobiles of all sizes and shapes were swarming around them. It was all kind of exciting, but Hunt would rather have been aboard the *Heinlein*. For one thing, he was wearing the same uniform he'd worn the day before and it was feeling a little gritty. He could stand it, but he didn't like it.

"Hungry?" Hunt asked.

Jan quickly admitted that he was. He leaped down from his bunk and began to search the ship. Eventually he found a locker full of small loose boxes of Sugar Slammers. "If that advertisement is any clue, we're supposed to eat this stuff in a bowl with milk."

"I guess we'll just have to eat it the hard way," Hunt said. He held up his hands, and Jan threw him a box. It had a picture of Commodore Edwards on the front panel. The box in Jan's hand featured Cadet Jolly. Hunt tore his open carefully, so as not to spill any of the contents.

"I'm hungry enough to eat it any way I can," Jan said. "Assuming I can eat it at all."

Each of them settled on an acceleration couch and pulled a handful of crunchies from his box.

"Not bad," Jan said as he chewed.

"A little sweet," Hunt remarked.

"Maybe it's better in a bowl with milk," Jan suggested.

"Maybe the youth of this era will eat anything if it has the right picture on the front of the packaging," Hunt said, making them both chuckle.

As they satisfied their hunger, their enthusiasm for the Sugar Slammers diminished. Hunt still had about a third of a box left when he decided he'd had enough.

"Coffee," Jan pleaded.

"Yeah," Hunt agreed, having no idea where they might get some, or if people even drank it in this era.

Eventually the machine pulled the ship into a big paved field marked off with what Hunt supposed were parking spaces. There was room for hundreds, maybe thousands, of automobiles. The machine pulled the ship through an open gate and into a wide area where a lot of people and trucks and equipment were waiting. It looked as if somebody had gone to a lot of trouble transferring the studio's storage area to this new location. He did not see the time machine, though he looked for it.

The machine stopped. The sudden silence was almost as loud as the motor had been.

"Here we go," Jan said. "What are you going to tell—" He was interrupted when somebody opened the door from the outside. Hunt attempted to erect a friendly smile on his face as he turned to the doorway.

CHAPTER 7

A FLIGHT TO THE MOON

A big guy wearing what looked like heavy-duty work clothes stared in at them. "What the..." he began in surprise.

"Problem, Bob?" a voice called from outside. It sounded familiar.

"What are you fellows doing in here?" Bob demanded.

Hunt was about to answer when Bob stepped away and a new face looked in. It belonged to Al, the man who'd taken them to dinner, *Space League's* writer.

Al was ready to be angry, but when he saw who was aboard the ship, he laughed. "You boys certainly get around," he said.

"Good seeing you too," Hunt said.

"Uh, nice ship," Jan said, holding up his end of the conversation.

"We take it with us when we make personal appearances. It gives the fans a thrill."

"I'm thrilled," Jan assured him.

"You better come out of there. The professionals need to give the ship a going over before we let the thundering hordes look around."

Once again Hunt wondered about Al's motives. He was letting them off easy, and without asking any questions. Hunt couldn't figure it out. When there weren't so many people around Hunt would have to take the initiative and ask *him* a few questions.

Once they were outside, five or six fellows hurried aboard the ship. "Come on," Al said, and led Hunt and Jan away.

They descended a short metal stairway to a large open area that was surrounded by strange spindly structures that towered over them from a great height and looked as if aliens might have built them—impossible, of course.

"What kind of place is this?" Jan asked.

"It's an amusement park," Al said. "People come here to have all kinds of experiences they can't have anywhere else." He glanced at them. "Don't you people have amusement parks where you come from?"

"Oh, sure," Jan said. "Ours are just a little different."

"A little," Hunt agreed. Jan had taken him to a famous park on Venus. It had been a nice change from the amusements he normally enjoyed, which were, for the most part, virtual. He was attacked by renegade Venusians, and rode a *scorps* around and around to the accompaniment of loud cheerful organ music—a simple ride, and of course none of the *scorps* were any more real than the renegade Venusians, but the experience was curiously satisfying.

"If you hang around long enough, you'll probably have a chance to go on some of the rides," Al promised.

"Wonderful," Hunt said, pretty sure he didn't mean it.

They strolled across the open area to a line of green benches. Relaxing on one of the benches, sipping something that smelled like—yes, like coffee—were Christopher Thrash and Eunice Quigley. Apparently she had been right not to worry about Garley taking her boyfriend away from her. Where was Garley, anyway?

Smiling, Thrash stood up and strode forward, leaving Eunice on the bench. She closed her eyes and raised her face to the sky as if attempting to get a tan—perhaps she was. Thrash shook hands with Hunt, Jan, and Al and welcomed them to Carnival Town.

"Is there any way we could get a cup of that coffee?" Jan asked.

"Of course," Thrash said, as if he were happy to do them an enormous favor. He raised his hand, and a young man about Hunt's age ran up to the group. After Thrash and the man conferred for a few seconds the man ran off, but he was back shortly carrying a tray holding two steaming paper cups. Hunt and Jan each took one. They sipped appreciatively.

"Al spoke of thundering hordes," Hunt said. "Where are they?"

"The park will open in an hour or so. Personally, I like the place better this way—though if we don't open we won't make any money." Thrash laughed pleasantly. "Come on. I'll show you around." He spoke to Eunice over his shoulder. "Come on, sweetie, I'll show you the sights."

She got up, smoothed her skirt—it was white and sprinkled with bright, candy-colored flowers—and joined them as they strolled into Carnival Town under a sign that would probably be pretty spectacular when lit at night.

"Where's Ms. Garley?" Hunt asked, as if the answer were of little consequence.

"She's perfectly fine," Thrash said.

"Oh?" Hunt said.

"You'll be seeing her soon," Thrash said. "Right now we have more important things to do."

"That's reassuring," Hunt said. "But it doesn't answer my question."

Thrash scowled. Al shook his head.

"We feel kind of responsible for her," Jan explained.

"That's good of you," Thrash said, "but entirely unnecessary." He glared at him for a moment but said no more before continuing his stroll with Eunice.

Hunt could see that arguing with Thrash would get him nowhere. If Garley really was safe, and they really would see her eventually, patience might be the big virtue here. If Thrash was lying about her condition, Hunt needed a plan, which at the moment he did not have.

The five of them continued their leisurely saunter along a wide street that seemed to go right up the center of the park. The place was beautifully landscaped with trees and colorful flowers. Lining the street were garish wagons identified with strange and interesting labels like "Miss Bushy, the Bearded Lady," "Muscles, the Strong Man," "Mr. Electro," and "Sssuzi, the Lizard Girl." There were also booths where people were preparing food of various kinds—sweet, spicy, sour, savory—the fragrances of which mixed appetizingly in the cool morning air. But the strongest odor was none of those; it was a hot smell that made Hunt think of the French fries he'd had the night before at the Shanghai Café. Without thinking, he raised his nose to inhale. Jan did the same.

"Ah yes, grease," Thrash remarked, and inhaled heavily. "It makes America strong."

"No doubt," Hunt remarked as they ambled along.

"Anybody want a hot dog?" Thrash asked.

"A what?" Jan asked.

"Uh, boss," Al said, "if you plan on taking us on the Moon Rocket Ride, maybe we should wait on the hot dogs."

Thrash frowned, but reluctantly agreed. "Pansies," he remarked under his breath, as if it were an insult.

"Moon Rocket Ride?" Hunt asked, hoping to change the subject but also curious. Unless his knowledge of history was way off, there were no ships going to the moon this year or any time soon. Of course, the Moon Rocket might be as fake as the *Magellan*, the ship he and Jan had ridden to Carnival Town.

"You'll see," Thrash said, and grinned. He liked his secrets, yes he did.

Soon the street opened up into an enormous open space where the alien structures were standing. Before, Hunt had been able to see only their tops, but now he could see them right down to the ground. The group walked past a structure circled by umbrella-like forms that could be hauled to the top closed, and then opened as they fell back to the ground. Another looked as if it would swing a small car—built to carry maybe two people, and designed to look like an airplane—around on long arms. A big vertical hoop with cars hanging all around the edge turned up and back a little, as if eager to begin. Small boats were lined up in a water-filled canal before a dark entrance identified as the Tunnel of Love. Each of the attractions had a small ticket booth out in front with a big sign saying what it was. Men and woman counted change and brought out thick disks of tickets.

But Thrash did not detain them at any of these places. They marched on until they reached a huge structure that seemed to be one narrow track curling and twisting and climbing and falling as if it were having a bad dream.

Thrash smiled and rocked up and back on his heels while looking at the construction, as pleased as if he'd built it with his own two hands. "The Moon Rocket Ride," he announced.

A man dressed in a work shirt and heavy pants stood at the bottom, with one hand resting on a thick lever that thrust out of a metal box big enough to hold Al's automobile. Behind him was a line of vehicles resting on the track. Each vehicle was a car that had three seats, one behind the other.

"Hello, boss," the man said and waved his ancient fedora at Thrash.

"All ready to go, Gary?" Thrash asked.

"You bet," Gary said.

"I was expecting a moon rocket," Jan said.

"Oh, we just call it that. We had to call it something," Thrash said enthusiastically. "Come on. I don't think you'll be disappointed." He helped Eunice into the front seat of the front car. Her jaw was clenched and she didn't look well.

Hunt was pretty sure he didn't want to do this any more than Eunice did. "Have a good time," he told Thrash, and took a step back.

"Not much of a sport, are you?" Thrash accused.

"I'll go," Jan piped up.

Jan surprised Hunt occasionally, and this was one of those times. Hunt sighed and decided it would be bad for morale if Jan went by himself. Maybe also bad for his relationship with Christopher Thrash, who seemed to be a pretty formidable guy—even more important than Al. He might be useful finding the time machine, if they ever had another chance to look for it.

"All right," Hunt said. "I feel like a sport all of a sudden."

Thrash got in next to Eunice and put his arm around her. She moved closer to him but did not snuggle. Gary pulled a metal bar back against their chests, then helped Hunt and Jan into the seat behind them and pulled their bar back. Al climbed into the third seat and pulled back the bar himself.

"Hang on tight, folks," Thrash cried out. "Blast-off, Gary."

"Right, boss." Gary pulled back on the big lever and the cars began to move.

Hunt gripped the bar as if his life depended on it, though at first the car moved so slowly that doing so seemed pointless. Some mechanism in the track made a loud clicking noise as the car climbed the first steep hill. Hunt was looking almost straight up into the sky. Gripping the bar now seemed wiser. Eunice was already burying her head in Thrash's shoulder. At the top of the hill the car paused for a second or two, and suddenly it was falling down the other side of the hill with the rush and noise of a plummeting spaceship. Wind beat against Hunt's face. The noise and beating continued as the car barreled around a steeply banked turn, then went around a turn the other way. More turns. More climbs and quick frightening descents during which Hunt yelled without meaning to and felt as if his stomach was about to fly out his mouth. He was too busy with his own terror to notice how Jan was taking all this. But Hunt knew he wasn't the only one yelling. Eunice screamed as if she were being murdered.

After what seemed like hours, the car returned to the ground and slowed as it approached the station where

Gary waited for it. He pulled back on his big lever and the car stopped with a jerk. Hunt felt as if he were still moving. The Moon Rocket Ride was much worse than riding in an automobile. He wanted to sit until he stopped trembling, but Gary was already helping him from the car. Hunt's legs were weak and his knees shook.

"I haven't been through anything like that," Jan said, "since one of those acceleration trials during my first year at the Academy." Like Hunt he was leaning against the car, looking a little greener than usual.

Hunt could only agree. He moved his finger in a pattern on his opposite uniform sleeve and saw that the ride hadn't lasted more than a few minutes.

Al was bearing up well, and Thrash was smiling as if the experience had not affected him at all except to excite him. Eunice, having aged about forty years, clutched Thrash's arm.

"Let's get that hot dog now," Thrash said as he glanced at Al. "If it's okay with you."

"Sure, boss," Al said. "But give me a minute to catch my breath." He laughed. "That attraction ought to be pretty popular with some people."

"Pansies," Thrash mumbled again. "You all right, angel?" he asked Eunice gently. She tried to smile and leaned on him as they walked away together, not moving very fast. Hunt, Jan, and Al followed.

Thrash bought each of them a paper cup full of a sweet brown sparkling liquid and a hot dog, which turned out to be a long dowel of spiced meat—colored a shade of red not found in nature—plopped into a slit in a small loaf of bread obviously designed to fit it, along with various condiments in bright shades of green and yellow. The hot dog was hot but looked nothing like a dog. The man selling the food tried to give it away—Thrash was the boss, after all—but Thrash insisted on paying the usual price for everything. The food-seller stared at him as if Thrash were some kind of saint. Maybe in his circle he was.

Like Jan, Hunt began to eat his hot dog and he found it tasty. In a few minutes they had all washed down their hot dogs with the brown liquid, which Thrash called soda pop.

While they sat on a bench in front of the hot dog stand, sucking on the ice remaining in their paper cups and picking the meat and bread out of their teeth, people began walking in along the main street from the front of the park. Couples strolled, kids ran, members of families marched along as if this was the most important job they would do today.

"Here they come," Al pointed out amiably.

Thrash got up and pulled Eunice to her feet. "Time to go to work." He studied Hunt and Jan. "Those uniforms aren't quite what Edwards and Jolly wear on the show," he went on to Al. "Do you think the fans will find them acceptable?"

"Most of them won't notice," Al assured him.

"All right, then, back to the ship."

CHAPTER 8

A SPECIAL BOY?

They hurried as best they could against the tide of the entering throng back to where the *Magellan* still rested on its skids. The machine that had pulled them to the park was gone, and a second hatch was open above a staircase near the nose of the ship. A huge crowd surrounded the ship, and men dressed in *Space League* uniforms were organizing the multitude into a line that snaked up and back, filling the open area next to the ship. The children were easier to work with than the adults, some of whom insisted that they knew somebody important and didn't have to wait. They didn't get anywhere with the security guys, who had obviously heard that story before. Christopher Thrash watched the scene for a moment, but didn't get involved. He let the security guys do their job.

"You gentlemen will have the honor of standing at the exit door where you will distribute boxes of Sugar Slammers to them that wants 'em, and most people will want 'em. Make sure that anyone who wants to enter the contest does so."

"Wait a minute," Jan began angrily. "We didn't..."

Thrash glared.

"We would love to help out," Hunt said quickly.

Thrash nodded as his face relaxed. "Get them started, Al," he said, and walked away, his arm through Eunice's as if he didn't have a care in the world.

"You're not going to make any friends that way," Al said to Jan. He escorted them up the stairs at the nose of the ship, and positioned them on either side of the open hatch next to a crate of Sugar Slammers. At the bottom of the staircase was a long table. Something that looked like a space helmet stood at one end, and a pile of cards and some pencils were at the other. Near the table stood one of the security guards.

"Give a box to every person who comes out. Got it?" Al said.

"I think so," Jan said. "Do you want to go through the instructions again?"

Al just laughed. "And tell them about the contest. All they have to do is fill out a card and drop it into the space helmet."

"What can they win?" Hunt asked.

"Lunch with our stars?" Al guessed. "A visit to the set? Autographed *Space League* books and toys? How the hell should I know? Maybe a year's supply of Sugar Slammers. Look, I have to go—got work of my own to do."

"You seem to do a little of everything," Hunt said.

"A little," Al agreed, and trotted down the steps.

"Just a minute," Hunt called, thinking this might be the right moment to ask a few probing questions.

Al turned back to look at Hunt, and Hunt was about to ask his questions when he noticed that the security guard at the contest table was also taking an interest.

"Nothing," Hunt said. "It'll wait."

"Okay," Al said. He wandered away and was soon lost in the crowd.

"I didn't go to System Guard Academy to pass out boxes of breakfast food," Jan said with irritation.

"It's all part of the job," Hunt told him, "just like running the power deck back on the *Heinlein*."

"Ah, the power deck," Jan said dreamily.

In a few moments people began to step out the front hatch: bright-eyed kids of all ages, adults who were either fascinated or too mature to take any of this theater seriously. Many discussed excitedly what they had seen inside the ship. Nobody turned down a box of Sugar Slammers. A few of the customers asked for another and got it. There seemed to be plenty of boxes, more than enough.

Time passed surprisingly quickly, and soon Hunt saw Thrash and Eunice at the other side of the big open space, strolling toward the ship. They eventually came to the table where many kids and a few adults were filling out cards and dropping them into the space helmet. Thrash had a long discussion with the security guy at the table, but it seemed to be friendly. Because she was out of costume, nobody paid any attention to Eunice Quigley, although she was the woman who played the Amethyst Queen.

Another little boy came out the hatch. Hunt blinked at him twice and poked Jan in the shoulder. He had turned away, getting another handful of Sugar Slammers boxes. When Jan saw the kid who had just emerged from the ship, he also blinked and stared. The kid was a chubby lad in his early teens wearing baggy blue pants and a collarless shirt with wide alternating red and blue horizontal stripes, but there was nothing really special about him.

He held out his hand, ready to take a box. Behind the boy more visitors were bunching up inside the ship.

CHAPTER 9

SLIPPERY SAM PEPPER

Thrash peered up at Hunt and Jan from the contest table and frowned. "Problem, boys?" he called up to them.

"No, sir," Hunt said and gave him the best grin he could manage.

"It's Andrew Gordon," Jan whispered to Hunt excitedly.

"Who?" Thrash asked as climbed the steps toward them.

Hunt had no doubt that Jan was right. It was Andrew Gordon, who in a few years would open a flying school that would eventually become System Guard Academy. Hunt would recognize Gordon anywhere. The Academy text recordings and historical records were full of photographs of him.

"I thought I knew him," Hunt told Thrash, "but I was wrong." He gave Gordon another box of Sugar Slammers and asked him to move along.

Thrash frowned as the kid descended the stairs. Like almost everyone else, he stopped at the contest table, filled out a card, and dropped it into the helmet.

"I hope I win," he said to no one in particular.

"I hope so too, son," Thrash said. Customers were once again pouring from the forward hatch and edging their way around Thrash.

Suddenly, several men separated themselves from the snaking line of customers on the open cement apron and began firing pistols into the air. Members of the crowd screamed and run around like insects in a disturbed ant-hill. Thrash's security men ran forward with their own weapons to cut out the armed men, herding them away from the customers.

Thrash dashed down the stairs, shouting orders, trying to get the situation under control. He wasn't armed, which made his attempt more difficult. At the contest table he grabbed the space helmet full of cards. Hunt couldn't guess why he would do that right now.

While Thrash's security men forced the attackers into a tighter and tighter bunch, adults swooped up children or grabbed the hands of the persons they'd come in with and ran for the exit. Many of the customers were crying.

"It looks as if Thrash's people need some help," Hunt cried. Jan rapidly followed him down the stairs and out into the emptying area around the ship.

A large man in a natty gray suit marched quickly toward Christopher Thrash with murder in his eye. He had narrow shoulders and a body the shape of an enormous tear drop, but that didn't prevent him from looking dangerous, especially with a pistol in one hand.

"I'll take that helmet," the large man said.

"How are you doing, Sam?" Thrash asked, as if they were friends meeting on the street.

Both Thrash and Sam snapped their heads around when one of the attackers fired his pistol in Hunt's direction; a bright outline flared around Hunt, instantly slowing the bullet, and it dropped to the pavement. Hunt fired back with the weapon in the cuff of his uniform shirt, striking the attacker with a shaft of purple light that seemed as solid as a harpoon. As he fell to the ground, he evaporated.

Though most of the customers were gone by now, Hunt and Jan kept moving and shooting at any attackers who had managed to avoid Thrash's security force.

A platoon of men in blue uniforms ran in through the gate. The uniforms looked something like the outfits worn by the guards who had been stalking Hunt and Jan the night before. More security men? The local police?

Once inside the big open area before the *Magellan*, they stopped and glanced around in confusion. Hunt and Jan fired more purple light harpoons and a dozen or so men in the blue uniforms moved toward the attackers. The rest of the policemen made a second ring around the corralled attackers and Thrash's security men.

The policemen did not fire at Hunt and Jan, so Hunt and Jan did not fire at them. They allowed themselves to be surrounded. One of the older policemen—if that's what they were—kept a close eye on Hunt and Jan while his colleagues patted them down for weapons.

"You can't do this to us," Jan protested.

"Take it easy, fellah," the older policemen advised. "Once we get you downtown you'll have a chance to tell your story."

"That ought to be interesting," Hunt said softly to Jan, who did not seem reassured.

"Well?" the senior policeman demanded of his under-lings when they stopped searching Hunt and Jan.

"Nothing," one of the clean-cut and efficient young policemen said.

"What do you mean, 'nothing?'"

"No weapon of any kind," he said. "Nothing that looks like a weapon, anyway."

Before the senior policeman could ask another question, Sam turned away from Thrash, apparently having no more interest in either him or the helmet. Instead, he waved at the *Magellan*, or perhaps to someone still aboard. Seconds later, a blast of fire erupted from the tail of the ship. Frantic voices hollered from inside, and Hunt and Jan hurried to help get the customers off the ship before something else happened. The last of them barely made it out before the ship scooted forward on its skids and gathered speed as it tilted off the flatbed and across the concrete. Hunt and Jan could not help watching as it crashed into the machine that had pulled the flatbed through traffic. The ship exploded, sending a fireball into the air, and making a boom so loud it echoed off mountains that were miles away.

Hunt glanced around and saw that Sam and his army were gone. The policemen were just noticing this too, and they ran for the gate in a mob. But they were too late. Somewhere out in the parking field the engines of many automobiles growled. The automobiles roared out of the big lot and forced their way into the traffic flow. The senior policeman ordered two automobiles full of his young associates to go after them.

"And don't come back alone," he called as the automobiles, sirens shrieking, followed the cars of the attackers.

Thrash marched with determination around the open cement apron, still clutching the space helmet full of cards. He ordered his own security men to see to the needs of the few guests who remained—some sitting on the ground, some on the green benches; some were crying, but most just stared at nothing, obviously still in shock from experiencing an attraction no one, not even Thrash, had expected to encounter that day.

Thrash approached Hunt and Jan, standing with a group of policemen. "Why are you holding these men, officer?" Thrash asked.

"Didn't you see the weapons they were firing?" one of the younger policemen asked. "Gosh, it was something."

"It's true," the first policeman said. "They have a lot of explaining to do. And maybe you do too. We didn't find anything on them."

"I can explain. I'm Christopher Thrash. I own this place."

"What do you know about those ray gun things?"

"Oh, that," Thrash waved a hand, as if the futuristic weapons were nothing. "I can explain that right now. We fire weapons like that all the time on our television show. It's what we call a special effect. You didn't find any weapons on them because they weren't carrying any."

"You mean these gentlemen are part of the show?"

"Sure. That's right. Firing those ray guns is part of their job here at the park. These fellows work for me. Why else would they be wearing those uniforms?"

"And do those fellows they shot at also work for you?"

A good question. Hunt couldn't wait to hear Thrash's answer.

"The ones who disappeared work for me."

"Oh? Tell me more."

"The disappearing is all done with stage magic. While you were distracted by the ray guns, they tore off their outer shirts and became part of the crowd. The others, the ones who managed to escape, work for Slippery Sam."

A good answer, Hunt thought, though entirely a fabrication. Anyone hit by the blast of a ray gun disappeared. So far none of the policemen had noticed.

"You mean Slippery Sam Pepper?" the policeman exclaimed.

"The same," Thrash admitted. "He and his gang attacked the park because he doesn't want me to succeed. He and I have always had a sort of personal feud."

The gray-haired policeman shrugged, and then gave the order not to bother about Hunt and Jan. "Let's go, boys," he called out. "Those men I sent after Sam Pepper's people are going to need some help."

Many members of the senior officer's force still seemed confused, but they hurried out after him and soon all the policemen were gone.

Thrash smiled as he watched them go. "I wish them luck, but they don't call him Slippery Sam for nothing."

CHAPTER 10

THE IMPORTANCE OF ANDREW GORDON

Thrash gave the order to let the guests back in. "Welcome, welcome," he called out. "Every attraction is free, today only."

Hunt and Jan followed Thrash as he marched past the burning pile of debris that had once been the *Magellan*, barely glancing at it, and back to the front hatch, where a short time before they had been handing out boxes of Sugar Slammers. Now, Eunice was just emerging from under the staircase.

"Thanks for the help," Hunt said.

Thrash ignored him. Instead of answering, he helped Eunice get settled on one of the steps. Her face was blank; she seemed too upset even to cry.

"Mr. Thrash?" Hunt asked again.

"What is it, Mr. Hunt?" Thrash said, though he kept looking at Eunice.

"How much of what you told the police was true?"

Thrash turned suddenly to look at him. "The part about Slippery Sam Pepper was mostly true," Thrash said. "The part about you gentlemen working for me was mostly not true. But I am very interested in learning more about your weapons."

"That's why you lied to the police about us working for you," Jan said.

"You are sharp," Thrash remarked appreciatively. "That is also why I am inviting you gentlemen to dinner this evening at my home in Beverly Hills. We'll have plenty of time to talk. Garley will be there, if that matters."

Did it matter? If he and Jan managed to get back to their own time, would they find it as they'd left it? Or had Garley already muddied the waters? Had he and Jan done the same without even trying? How changed would their own time be? Could they still stop her if they needed to?

"Fine," Hunt said. "It will be good to see her again."

Thrash huddled with his security men one more time, collected Eunice, and with the space helmet under one arm, led the way out to the field where all the automobiles were parked.

"Nobody else entering the contest?" Jan asked.

"I think I already have a winner," Thrash assured him.

That didn't seem fair to Hunt, but he wasn't in charge.

More automobiles arrived all the time. Great crowds of customers poured in at the front gate; word must have spread that all attractions were free that day. Thrash smiled at everybody and welcomed them boisterously until he and the others came to a sleek silver automobile with four doors, and enough room inside for team sports. Thrash invited Hunt and Jan to get into the back. Eunice rode up front holding the space helmet. Thrash started the engine, and as he backed out of his space, twisted a knob. Bouncy music poured from a grille in the control panel.

Hunt felt a little sick, as he had in Al's automobile—he did not enjoy the ride to Beverly Hills. As time went on, he felt steadier, but he still didn't think that riding in an automobile would ever be his favorite mode of transportation. And because he was in the back seat and Thrash had turned up the music, conversation was difficult at best. Hunt would have to wait until they arrived at Thrash's mansion before he learned anything new about the time machine or what Garley's plan might be.

Jan watched with interest as Hunt made a pattern over the left cuff of his uniform shirt with his right index finger, turning on the percepticon. The read-out glowed.

"We're getting farther away from the time machine," Jan said softly.

Hunt nodded.

"What's that?" Thrash called.

"Just admiring the architecture," Hunt said.

As they traveled, the streets became wider and cleaner. The sunshine seemed brighter, as if it were of higher quality than the light used at the other end of town. The décor on the buildings became more tasteful—in Hunt's futuristic opinion, anyway. Thrash turned off the main street he'd been on and roared up into the hills along a narrow twisting road hemmed in on both sides by high gleaming white walls, and by neatly trimmed hedges. He stopped at a driveway where a man in a suit opened a gate—a big metal spider web—to let the car in. The man in the suit gave Thrash a two-finger salute as the car entered.

The car swept along a wide curve of driveway and stopped under a stone canopy carved with faces that had bugged-out eyes, pointed ears, and long sharp tongues. A huge wooden door creaked as it opened on side hinges, and Al came out.

"I heard you fellows had quite a morning," he said as he ushered them into the front hall—a big room long enough to hold the *Magellan*. The wall-to-wall midnight blue carpeting was decorated with a complicated pattern of leaves and flowers and it was thick enough to hide gophers. At the back were two staircases leading up to a balcony, one on each side of a piece of stained-glass fantasy that took up the entire rear wall and let in plenty of light. It was a scene of medieval lords and ladies having lunch on the grass. They were having a swell time. One of the ladies was feeding a carrot to a unicorn.

"Slippery Sam," Thrash confirmed with disgust. "I should have expected he'd try something funny. This little attack is just one more mark against him." He took the space helmet from Eunice. "Why don't you go up to your room and take a nap before dinner?"

Eunice nodded, pecked him on the cheek, and toddled off.

He gave the helmet to Al. "Wait in the library. I'll be in shortly to tell you what to do with this." Al nodded and hurried along the hall to a side room. The door closed behind him with a polite click.

"What *are* you going to do with it?" Jan asked.

"I may tell you one of these days," Thrash said as he left them. When he ducked inside the library the latch didn't quite catch behind him and the door swayed slightly ajar.

A very tall, thin man dressed in striped pants and a black coat stepped gingerly along the hall. There wasn't much flesh on his face. He could have been the butler in a haunted house. "I am Stone," the tall man said with a surprisingly resonant voice. "I will show you gentlemen to your rooms." He bowed and led them away.

As they passed the slightly open door, Hunt saw Al sitting at a big desk sorting prize cards he'd taken from the space helmet. Hunt caught the name "Andrew Gordon" just before someone quickly shut the door.

Stone, Hunt, and Jan went up the stairs to the balcony, and from there to the second floor, a long, dim, door-lined corridor where sound died among padded straight-backed chairs placed at intervals against the wall, and was soaked up by heavy curtains and more thick carpeting. Between the doors were paintings of cottonwood groves, eucalyptus trees, and cliffs above the ocean.

Stone took each of them to a room of his own. He made sure they were comfortably settled, then went away. Hunt was relieved and a little surprised when he tried the door and found it wasn't locked. He turned and studied his room. It looked old-fashioned to him, which may have meant only that it was typical of the period: a fancy rug on the floor, some nice pieces of wooden furniture, and a bed that could have held three or four good friends. There was a bathroom rigged with ancient plumbing that made Hunt long for Freddy back on the *Heinlein*. A knock sounded at the door and Jan entered without waiting for Hunt to answer. Jan made himself at home in one of the big chairs.

"You look satisfied," Hunt said, considering him from the bathroom door.

"Just comfortable at last," Jan said. "Did you hear what Al said as we passed the library?" he asked.

"'Andrew Gordon,'" Hunt said. "Thrash probably overheard his name when you mentioned it to me on the stairs back at the *Magellan*."

"Could be," Jan admitted. "But why would that be important to Thrash?"

Hunt saw no reason why Jan was the only one who should be comfortable. He sat down in a rocking chair on the other side of the room and rocked a few times before he got the hang of it.

"I think my grandmother had one of those," Jan remarked.

"No doubt," Hunt said. "Let's try to focus here. Why do you think Gordon's name was important to Thrash?"

"Can't imagine." Jan snapped his fingers. "Unless it has something to do with Garley. Besides us, she is the only person who would attach any importance to that name."

"I'll buy that," Hunt said. "But why would it be important to Thrash?"

Jan gnawed on the knuckle of his right thumb and then frowned. "And why would he bother to go through the prize cards in the helmet?"

"To get Andrew Gordon's address?" Hunt suggested. "After all, they don't have access to Freddy."

"And they'd want his address because?" Jan prompted.

"I think that Thrash and Garley are plotting something together."

"And that is?"

"No idea."

They both stared at the rug in the center of the room. Hunt imagined Garley standing on the colorful geometric pattern, leaning over Dr. Eignberger's time machine, about to play with the control rods because she wanted to see if the time machine actually worked. Ghosts of clues. The imaginary scene was just something to look at while he thought.

"We know that Garley hates the System Guard," Hunt said at last. "And that Thrash was impressed by our weapons."

"How does that go with Andrew Gordon, who at this point in history is a child who eats Sugar Slammers?"

Hunt shrugged. "Good question. One of the best. I suspect that Thrash will give us the answer eventually."

"You think we're part of the plan he's plotting with Garley?"

"Us and our weapons."

Jan nodded. He looked worried.

CHAPTER 11

ALL IN THE SAME BOAT

"Come on," Hunt said as he stood up, "let's get some air."

Still looking worried, Jan leaped to his feet as if his spine were a spring and followed Hunt out the door. They nodded at Stone, who was arranging flowers in a vase on a table next to the stairs, and he nodded back. No one they met on their way outside took more than a polite interest in them—not even the occasional gorilla security man who was obviously not there for his looks or for his intelligence.

Once outside they wandered down a brick path that led them through a garden, and then along another brick path that crossed it. They sat for a few minutes listening to the musical tinkle of falling water in the fountain in the center of a small wooden building with open sides. Jan started to fidget. He soon got up and marched through a copse of fir trees. Having nothing better to do, Hunt followed him. When Jan came to a high stone wall, he smiled.

"What?" Hunt asked.

Jan made a pattern with his finger on the opposite cuff of his shirt and slowly rose, walking his fingers up the wall to guide himself.

"What are you doing?" Hunt asked.

"Escaping," Jan said, as if the fact should have been obvious.

"To where, for instance? We have only the vaguest idea where the time machine is, and an even more vague idea how to get there. Besides, we still have to find out exactly what Garley has in mind and then stop her."

Jan grumbled, but he stopped rising. One of the big men, looking more like a gorilla than ever, came by and looked up at him with mild curiosity. "Can I help you gentlemen?" he asked.

"Just looking around," Hunt said as Jan sank quickly to the ground.

The big man watched this performance as if he saw men floating in the air every day. "Of course," he said. "I think Mr. Thrash would like it if you returned to the house now."

"If Mr. Thrash would like it," Jan said, "it's fine with us."

Hunt and Jan walked back more or less the way they had come, with the big man making no attempt to hide as he followed them. The big man did not go in after them as they entered a side door. Hunt imagined there were plenty of people inside who would keep an eye on them.

It was a long afternoon, giving them time to explore the house—a mansion, actually—and they did so. Nobody was in the library when Jan knocked. Apparently, Thrash and Al had finished whatever they'd been doing because the prize cards and the space helmet were gone too. Hunt and Jan browsed among the books for a while, enjoying the pleasant but unfamiliar sensation of feeling and smelling and reading real books printed on paper. They had a few laughs over the predictions in the popular science magazines. Later they found a game room; the walls were divided into beautiful oblong wooden panels, each of which looked a little like a door. Soon Hunt and Jan were joined by one of the big security men who taught them to play pool. Hunt found that he was pretty good at it, applying what he knew about impact, velocity, and momentum.

The sun was low in the sky, casting long curtains of yellow light at an angle across the game room as Hunt lined up his next shot. Al casually entered the game room and suggested that the security man get himself a cup of coffee. "I'll watch 'em," Al said, nodding his chin at Hunt and Jan. Hunt didn't know what was going on, but he was willing to wait in order to find out.

The security man looked uncertain, then shrugged and left, closing the door gently but firmly behind him. Hunt, Jan, and Al contemplated each other. It was pretty obvious to all of them that he wasn't there to play pool or even to stop them from escaping. Why he *was* there Hunt could not yet guess.

"If you boys really wanted to escape," Al said conversationally, "you could probably find a way. Thrash has many enemies who might attack him here at home, so the mansion is riddled with secret doors, passages, and other escape routes."

"Where?" Jan asked.

"That's not important right now," Al assured him. "You'll find them when the time comes."

"When—" Jan began.

Hunt interrupted Jan. "Want to chalk up a cue?" he asked Al. There was no point interrogating Al if he wasn't in the mood to talk. Anyway, looking for one of those secret doors might be fun.

"Not particularly," Al said. "Though I don't object to playing if you're eager."

Hunt stood his cue in the rack and settled into one of the padded leather chairs scattered around the room. He laced his fingers across his stomach. Jan sat on the edge of the pool table swinging one leg. They both looked at Al expectantly.

"I suppose you can guess why you're here," Al said.

"Sure," Jan said. "Thrash wants to talk to us. He told us so himself."

Al nodded. "Do you want to talk to him?"

"We don't long for it," Hunt admitted. "But it may be difficult not to."

"Yeah," Al agreed. "He can be pretty persuasive if he wants to be. What about Garley?"

"What about her?" Jan asked.

"She's from the future too, isn't she?"

"What do you mean, *too*?" Hunt asked coolly, as if it really didn't matter.

Al smiled. "Those uniforms didn't come off any rack I know of."

"If we were from the future," Hunt asked, "how would we get here, er, now? You know what I mean."

"Better than you can guess, mister. I hear that tachyons would do the trick."

"All right." Hunt sat up. "Let's stop beating around the bush," he said. "In this year there is only one person in the world who would know about tachyons. The word was coined in 1967 by Gerald Feinberg—a good ten years from now, maybe more. It's in all the reference publications."

Jan's eyes got big as the implication of what Hunt had just said occurred to him.

Al remained calm. "And who would that one person be?" he asked.

"That would be Albert Covington, who was sent back in time by Dr. Edward Eignbergen using his shiny new time machine."

The game room was quiet for a minute.

"Sure," Jan said, "a guy from the future might have a little sympathy for other fellows stuck in the same boat. He was just too helpful, wasn't he?" Jan added to Hunt.

"I'm just a big softy," Al admitted.

"Do you know where our time machine is now?" Hunt asked.

"I can make an educated guess or two. You want to go home, I suppose."

"I suppose we do," Jan agreed. "Not to mention wanting to stop Garley from doing whatever dirty work she has planned."

"Not to mention," Hunt said, "I'd like to show Andrew Gordon what happens in the future because he starts his flying school."

That startled Al. "Is that a good idea?" he asked.

"It couldn't hurt," Jan said.

"That remains to be seen," Hunt said, genuinely curious to see what would happen. "You know what a percepticon is?" he asked.

"I do." Al admitted.

"Have a look at this." Hunt got up, and showed Al the cuff of his shirt. He did something above the cuff with a finger of his other hand, and the percepticon gave him the general direction and distance to the nearest tachyon—which meant to the nearest time machine. "Do those bearings mean anything to you?" Hunt asked.

"They mean my first educated guess was correct. The time machine is probably at Stormfield Storage. It's downtown. That's where Thrash stores things he wants to keep if there's no room for them in his mansion."

"The thing that bothers me," Jan said, "is that there ought to be two tachyon locations: one for our time machine, and one for yours."

"I was just getting to that," Hunt said. He and Jan stared at Al, waiting for him to explain if he could.

Al didn't seem bothered by the question. "It's simple enough," he said. "Pretty soon after I got here, the machine kinda sorta exploded."

"You mean it blew up?" Jan asked excitedly.

"That's exactly what I mean, junior. Ka-blooy. Nothing left, not so much as a tachyon molecule. So you see, I couldn't go home even if I wanted to."

"I guess we were lucky," Jan said.

"Dr. Eignbergen probably improved the Mark II," Al suggested. "He is—will be—a pretty smart fellow."

"You could return home with us," Hunt said. "*If* we had our machine."

Al shook his head. "Truth is," he said, "I have come to like the mid-1950s."

Hunt hoped he didn't like the 1950s so much that he wouldn't help them find their time machine. He'd been pretty helpful so far, but every man has his limits. Hunt wondered what Al's were.

Stone entered without knocking, his thin boney face as creepy as ever. "Dinner is being served in the dining room," he said with no more emotion than an announcer at a spaceport informing unfortunate travelers of a scheduling change.

Hunt had no idea where the dining room was. "We'll need a native guide," he said.

"Very well," Stone said, not sounding happy about it, not sounding any way at all.

Hunt and Jan thanked Al for showing them the fine points of pool. "I'll be off then," Al said. "I see you're in good hands."

Stone watched as Al left the room and closed the door behind him. "Shall we go?" he asked.

CHAPTER 12

DINNER WITH THE WINNER

Al was nowhere to be seen when Hunt and Jan followed Stone from the room. He led them down one of the two staircases to the main floor, then through a short hallway, at the end of which was a pair of sliding doors. He pushed the doors aside and bowed as he indicated that the two cadets should enter.

The people already seated stared at Hunt and Jan with interest. Thrash sat at one end of the long table—beautifully set with bright utensils and very elegant place settings—and Eunice sat at the other. Under a chandelier that looked as if it was made of diamonds, a white tablecloth ran between them like a fall of new snow. On one side sat the boy they had recognized at Carnival Town as Andrew Gordon; he was sandwiched between an older man and woman who were probably his parents. Andrew looked so excited he could barely stay in his seat, but his parents—if that was who they were—just looked uncomfortable. They kept glancing at Thrash—either trying to guess what he was thinking, or hoping for clues on how to act.

In the center of the other side of the table, Garley sat all alone. Hunt was surprised to see that she no longer wore the prospector's outfit they'd found her in, or even something a mid-twentieth century woman might wear.

She was dressed in the cloak, headdress, and makeup of the Amethyst Queen. She was smiling, lizard-like, to herself. Hunt would not want anyone to smile at him like that—especially if she fancied herself the evil ruler of outer space.

Each of the adults had a glass of wine, though it looked as if Mr. and Mrs. Gordon had not touched theirs. Andrew had a tumbler of milk. There was an enormous vase of flowers in the center of the table, and a dish of vegetables at each end: stalks of celery stuffed with something white and heaps of moist tiny red spheres, olives wrapped in bacon, and a bowl of assorted nuts.

Thrash smiled at Hunt and Jan. "Come in, come in, gentlemen," he called out as he gestured at them, encouraging them to enter.

Hunt and Jan strolled in and sat on either side of Garley. She ignored them.

"How are you doing, Miss Garley?" Hunt asked.

"I am well, thank you," she said in the formal tones of the Amethyst Queen, as if it was none of their business and she did not care if they knew it.

After a few seconds, Stone came back leading a line of maids dressed in formal black and white, each carrying a platter or a covered dish. Jan inhaled deeply and smiled. There was a salad, and chunks of meat in a pungent sauce. One of the platters held fat slices of crusty bread slathered in garlic butter. The maids set the platters and dishes on the table, and Stone adjusted them minutely.

"I thought we'd get a little fancy tonight," Thrash said with pleasure, "because we're celebrating the fact that Andrew won the space helmet drawing."

"What is that delightful smell?" Mrs. Gordon asked.

"Just like home," Jan remarked. Hunt hoped he wouldn't start talking about Venus.

"*Boeuf Bourguignon*," Thrash answered. "One of my favorite dishes. Please help yourselves."

As Mrs. Gordon scooped meat chunks onto Andrew's plate, which he ignored, he looked at Thrash hopefully with big, eager eyes. "What did I win? You didn't tell me yet."

"Win? Why, my boy, you won the best prize ever. I'm going to give you a part on *Space League*."

"Oh, my gosh," Andrew exclaimed with disbelief.

"Andrew has never acted before," Mr. Gordon admitted as if a little afraid that Thrash had not thought of this himself, and would now choose a different winner.

"No matter," Thrash said. "He's a bright boy. He'll pick it up."

He might pick it up, Hunt thought, or he might not; Hunt didn't believe it mattered. It was no coincidence that Andrew Gordon had won the contest. How Andrew Gordon was involved in Garley's plot, Hunt wasn't yet sure, but that he *was* involved was certain. The plot also had something to do with the time machine and the weapons Thrash had seen him and Jan use at the amusement park. Garley and Thrash, both now with lizard smiles, seemed as satisfied as if they'd won the Lunar Sweepstakes.

Hunt didn't think that Eunice had anything to do with their plot—she seemed more interested in the food. She'd already had two glasses of wine and Stone was pouring her a third.

"Do you like airplanes?" Hunt asked Andrew. It was a shot in the dark, but it might hit something.

"How did you know?" Andrew asked, delighted.

"You look like that sort of boy," Hunt said.

"Anyway, I did like airplanes," Andrew said, "but now I think I might take acting lessons. What do you say?" He looked from one parent to the other.

His mother smiled nervously.

"We'll see," his father said in a tone that always meant "no." It was obvious that neither of them thought of acting as honest work.

"Don't worry," Thrash confided to Andrew. "I'll talk to your parents." He chuckled as if this were a private joke.

Thrash and Andrew continued their discussion about the parts he might play on *Space League*, turning over the finer points of *Space League* plot, character, and science. As far as Hunt was concerned, they might as well have been speaking in Old High Martian. Andrew's parents tried to be agreeable, but didn't actually say much. Garley said even less, but watched Andrew and Thrash closely with obvious delight, like a cat waiting at a mouse hole. Eunice just drank.

There was a pause after the main course was finished, when everybody just sat and digested, anaconda-style. Maids brought out coffee along with a spectacular dessert composed of grilled fruit on long skewers, covered with a sweet brown sauce and accompanied by vanilla ice cream. With Thrash's encouragement, Andrew had three helpings while his mother looked on with disapproval. Mr. Gordon drank his coffee glumly, obviously not liking the relationship growing between his son and these show people, but also not having the nerve to go up against Mr. Thrash.

"Those are great uniforms," Andrew said to Hunt and Jan, "But they don't look like the ones on *Space League*."

"We're thinking of redesigning the uniforms," Thrash told him. "We can probably get you one like it. What do you think?"

"Wow!" Andrew exclaimed.

"Meanwhile, I'd like to talk a few things over with your parents—you know, grown-up stuff. Necessary but actually pretty dull."

Hunt saw an opening. "Let's go up to the game room," he said. "Jan and I will tell you all about the uniforms." What he said was even true to a certain extent.

Thrash's eyes narrowed, making him look wild and menacing. "Get Al," he demanded of one of the maids. She immediately went out and returned a few minutes later with Al, who looked eager to comply with anything. "Show Andrew to the game room. Teach him a few games."

Garley shook hands with Andrew and wished him "spaceman's luck." Everybody smiled and waved as Al escorted Andrew from the dining room.

While that was going on, Eunice slid down in her seat and began snoring like a sea lion. Hunt sipped his coffee, but it was cold and he put his cup down.

"Please excuse me," Thrash said to Mr. and Mrs. Gordon. "I have some things to discuss with Hunt and Jan. Mr. Llewelyn will take good care of you. He's a very fine lawyer."

As if summoned by magic, a solid-looking man in a dark suit and a shirt that gleamed as if it were radioactive entered the dining room and unrolled a professional smile across the table. "Sorry I missed dinner," he said in a voice as deep as space itself. "Will you join me in the library, Mr. and Mrs. Gordon? We have a few details concerning your son's contract to discuss."

They looked confused by the sudden change in plans, but they went.

"Well," Garley said when they were gone, "that's over with."

"Charming people," Thrash said, and asked the world at large for more hot coffee.

"Now that we're more or less alone," Hunt said, "maybe you can tell us what you really have in mind."

"Maybe," Jan said as if he didn't believe it would ever happen.

CHAPTER 13

WHAT'S IN IT FOR THEM

"Stone, would you see that Eunice gets to bed all right?" Thrash said.

Stone and one of the maids got Eunice to her feet and half dragged her from the room.

Garley and Thrash looked at each other, small smiles playing around their lips like friendly puppies. "Well?" Hunt asked, hoping they would take the hint to begin.

"Yes," Thrash said, "it's time." He leaned forward on his elbows, getting chummy with Hunt and Jan. "I was very impressed with the weapons you used on Slippery Sam's people," he said as if he were letting them in on a big secret.

"Special effects, you told the police," Jan said.

"I did," Thrash admitted. "But I know just as you do that's not true. Those weapons are from the future and so are you boys." He sat back in his chair, ready to enjoy the effect this revelation would have on Hunt and Jan.

Neither Hunt nor Jan made a remark. Their faces showed no reaction. They were not ready to admit anything.

"Lighten up, boys," Garley said. "I told him how we got here. Denying it will do you no good."

Hunt nodded. If he hadn't seen the weapons in action, Thrash might not have believed her. But as things stood,

Hunt was pretty sure they couldn't fool Thrash any longer. "What's in this for you?" he asked.

Garley took a long sip of wine and a deep breath. "You know I don't like the System Guard," she said at last.

"Despite the fact that two Guard cadets saved your life," Hunt reminded her.

Thrash laughed, causing Garley to frown. "I suppose that makes everything all right," she said sarcastically.

"If not all right, then you might at least give us the benefit of the doubt," Jan said.

Garley opened her mouth to answer that, but Hunt interrupted her. "I think we get it," he said. "You hate the System Guard. Can we move on? What has that to do with Andrew Gordon?"

"You've been to the Academy," Garley pointed out angrily, "had all the history courses, heard all the propaganda, been fully indoctrinated. You know that when he gets older or got older or will get older—Dr. Eignbergen will need to invent some new tenses along with his time machine—Andrew Gordon will start a flying school that eventually will become the System Guard Academy."

Hunt had a bad feeling about this, but he plunged in with a guess: "But now that he's won the contest, he is more interested in acting than in flying."

"That's right, big boy. I was going to just kill him, but Mr. Thrash suggested a less messy way to stop him."

Thrash nodded. "I can be violent if I must," he admitted, "but it is never my first choice."

"What is your first choice?" Hunt asked. He was getting tired of going around in circles.

Thrash ignored Hunt's question and looked directly at Garley, eye to eye, as if he were trying to hypnotize her.

"Tell him, dear," Thrash said, "Tell him what's in it for you."

"Merely the non-existence of the Academy. It will never be founded," Garley said, enjoying the prospect. "Thrash already helped me accomplish that by allowing Andrew Gordon to win the contest."

"And in return," Jan said, "You promised him weapons from the future. That ought to put Mr. Thrash way ahead of Slippery Sam, and the police too."

"I am confident," Thrash said agreeably.

"What do you need us for?" Hunt asked.

"I was wondering the same thing," Thrash said. He stared at Garley, waiting for an answer.

She frowned and shifted in her seat. Hunt, Jan, and Thrash watched her calmly, as if she were an exhibit. She would have to tell them something eventually. The only question was whether or not it would be the truth.

"I don't know how to operate the time machine," she confessed, then hurried on. "That's why I encouraged you to get your hands on Hunt and Jan. They saw the inventor operate it. They can get your weapons for you. I owe you that much."

"You have some nerve," Thrash said admiringly.

"I do," Garley said, suddenly sparkling with delight.

"All right," Hunt said. "I'm glad we're all friends again. But neither of you counted on one thing."

"And that is?"

"Jan and I will not help you."

"I thought as much," Thrash said. "But I am not without my persuasive methods."

"We can guess your methods," Jan said.

"Of course you can. And you probably are not frightened by them. I've dealt with you hero types before." Thrash didn't seem bothered by this.

"Even if we wanted to help you," Hunt suggested, "it might not be possible. If the Academy really is gone because Andrew went into acting instead of flying, the uniforms we're wearing will look pretty suspicious in our home time. Where would we get the weapons you want?"

"There are always weapons," Thrash said. "The System Guard wouldn't have them all."

"We still won't help you," Jan said, making it sound like a threat.

"Andrew Gordon is just a kid," Thrash said. "I'd hate to see him hurt."

"I wouldn't," Garley muttered.

Thrash shook his head at that. He spoke to one of the maids, who had been standing near the door to the kitchen. "Get Stone," he told her. She acknowledged his order and went out. A few minutes later she came back with Stone, his face the usual blank carving.

"Take these two to the game room," Thrash ordered. "Al and Andrew are already there. Give Hunt and Jan some time to get to know Andrew better, to get to like him and maybe to feel a little protective. I want them to think about all that before I need to start the rough stuff."

"I'll start it for you," Garley said.

"Shut up," Thrash ordered, suddenly sounding tired and disgusted.

Both Hunt and Jan enjoyed Garley's discomfort when she looked at Thrash with surprise. They marched after Stone as he escorted them back to the game room. The door was closed, but Stone opened it without knocking.

Hunt and Jan entered, interrupting Andrew in the middle of a shot at the pool table.

"Hi," Andrew said. He smiled, glad to see them again.

Stone nodded, then left, closing the door behind him.

When Stone was gone, Hunt looked around at his fellow conspirators. "I think we'd better go," he said.

CHAPTER 14

ANDREW BEGINS TO UNDERSTAND

"Huh?" Andrew said.

"Don't say 'huh,'" Jan said. "It's vulgar."

"Huh?" Andrew said again.

"I told you—" Jan began.

"Drop it," Hunt ordered, interrupting him. "We're going to take you to the future, Andrew. You'll learn more about these uniforms than you ever thought possible."

Andrew seemed confused. Hunt could tell that he wanted to say, "huh?" again, but he fought it.

"Pay attention," Al said to Hunt and Jan. "You're about to learn all you want to know about Mr. Thrash's secret passages." He knocked twice on one of the door-sized panels in the wall, causing it to slipped aside. He was about to lead the others through into the dim passage beyond when a low electronic whine began and a pale blue bubble grew in the center of the room. The surface of the bubble reflected Andrew and the three men watching. Inside the bubble was a vague and ghostly vision of two people and Dr. Eignbergen's time machine. The whine got louder and the vision solidified. Suddenly the bubble burst to reveal another Andrew, this one much more relaxed than the one already in the room. Standing next to him was another Al. He was smiling despite the fact he looked as if somebody had shot him in the shoulder with a blaster on low power. The time machine stood between them.

Voices from the hallway fell into the stunned silence. "It'll all work out," Thrash was saying, "You'll see. We're dealing with heroes, after all. Nothing is more predictable."

"Heroes," Garley said with contempt. She sounded as if she was just outside the door.

Hunt hustled the others out through the secret door. The Al who had opened it was the last to leave. He saluted the Al who had just arrived, stepped into the corridor, and slid the door closed. Hunt hoped that he'd manage to get the panel closed before Thrash and Garley entered the room, but didn't want to check to find out. Al led Hunt, Jan, and Andrew from one dusty branch of the secret passage to another.

They emerged outside the wall that surrounded Thrash's mansion, and Al brought them to his small yellow automobile, which was not far away. Andrew took the seat next to Al, while Hunt and Jan climbed into the back.

"I hate this," Jan grumbled.

"I did too," Al said, "but I got used to it. Cars are what the twentieth century is all about." He raced the engine, and a moment later they were on their way down the hill.

"Where are we going?" Andrew asked.

"Downtown," Al said. "We have to pick up the time machine."

"But wasn't that a time machine we saw in the game room?"

Jan chuckled. "Go ahead, Al," he said, "Explain it to him."

"Time travel is a funny thing," was all Al said.

Andrew turned and looked to Hunt and Jan for help.

"It's difficult to explain," Hunt said. "But after you've been to the future and back once I think you'll understand."

"And don't say, 'huh?'" Jan ordered.

"I wasn't going to. I was going to ask about Mr. Thrash and my parents. They'll be worried when I'm not in the game room. Al won't be there either."

"But you are there," Hunt reminded him. "You and Al just arrived with the time machine."

"I guess that kid in the time machine looked like me." Andrew didn't sound sure.

"It was you," Hunt said. "A you who had been to the future and back."

"Is that where we're going now?" Andrew asked. "To the future and back?"

"That's it, kid," Al said.

"See," Jan said, "you're beginning to understand already."

Andrew pursed his lips and wrinkled his brow, thinking hard. "So when me and Al go to the future and back, we'll be the ones in the game room—right? I'll go home with my parents, but Al will still have to explain why he let you two go."

Al laughed at that.

"You noticed our uniforms," Hunt said. "They are equipped with weapons. You may have noticed that we injured Al, or will injure Al, just enough to convince Mr. Thrash that Al tried to stop us from escaping but couldn't."

Jan suddenly turned and looked out the back window. "Do you think Thrash is following us?" he asked.

"Probably not," Al said. "He doesn't need us anymore. In his game room we left a time machine and somebody with enough nerve to try operating it."

"That would be Ms. Bernadette Garley," Jan guessed. "Even on short acquaintance, she seems like the type we can count on to have the nerve to do what she wants without thinking it over very much. Her nerve is how we got into this mess."

Hunt nodded. "If Thrash and Garley get lucky with the settings on that machine, they might be waiting for us when we get to the future. They might have been there a while, could be months, giving her a chance to cause plenty of trouble for the Academy. And he might be very busy acquiring weapons. In any case, we'll have to watch our step when we get home."

"I never thought of all that," Al said appreciatively. "Maybe you should be writing *Space League* episodes."

"Nobody would believe them," Hunt said. He tried to straighten it all out in his mind as he watched the city pass.

As they approached the center of the city, the buildings that lined the street got taller and darker. The pale streetlamps atop cement columns didn't help, only somehow making everything look older and more worn. People in old dilapidated clothes, many of them pushing wire wagons full of junk, shuffled along and lounged in doorways.

"I guess Thrash must trust you," Hunt said.

"Why is that?"

"He sent you to watch over the three of us. Apparently it didn't occur to him that you'd help us escape."

"Yeah, well, I've never before had a chance to help some fellows from my own time. This seemed like my big opportunity. Thrash might have played his hand differently if he'd known I was from the future too."

"I bet Dr. Eignbergen will like to see you when you get back to the future," Jan said.

"I bet he will. I'm sure he has a few questions for me. I don't mind answering them, but I'm not going to stick around. I've kind of gotten used to the mid-twentieth century."

"Besides," Jan said, "you already went through the cycle once. What do you think it would do to the space-time continuum if you didn't go back with Andrew?"

"I have no idea."

"Nobody does," Hunt said. "Let's keep it that way."

Soon the yellow automobile was booming through a deserted industrial neighborhood full of ugly, unadorned, windowless buildings—warehouses. Al pulled into a large empty parking field next to one of the larger structures. It looked big enough to house three or four ships the size of the *Heinlein*. In the side facing the parking field was a metal door illuminated by a single shaded bulb. A painted sign over the door said, "Stormfield Storage" in neat white letters.

"I hope you have a key," Jan remarked.

"Of course I do," Al said. "Thrash owns the building." He chuckled way down in his chest. "And he trusts me."

CHAPTER 15

WHERE TO?

They all got out of the automobile and walked to the door together. Al used a key on a ring bristling with keys to turn the lock; something inside the lock made a loud thunk when it fell back, and the door swung open easily, without a sound. Al felt around inside next to the door and flicked a switch that lit the whole place.

A corridor extended the length of the building, and more of them crossed that one at intervals. Each corridor was painted white, but they were scarred by black skid marks on the floors and walls that looked like the writing of some alien language Hunt had not seen before. Long tubes of bright light stretched down the ceiling in each corridor. Every few feet there was a door with number stenciled on to it in black paint. A small heavy mechanism, obviously a lock of some kind, hung just below the handle of each door. The building had been hard used.

Behind them the metal door closed slowly until it clicked.

"Which way?" Al asked.

Hunt looked at the percepticon read-out on his shirt cuff. It was flashing quickly now. "That way," he said, and strode down one of the corridors. The others followed.

The place had the atmosphere of a mausoleum. The air seemed dead, and the smell of dust and very old chemicals—and perhaps of the white paint that seemed to be everywhere—didn't help. The only sounds were those that they themselves were making. After a while the brightness of the light became oppressive.

Soon the flashing of the percepticon slowed. "What's wrong?" Al asked.

"It's above us," Hunt said as he waved his arm around to see where the reading was strongest.

"To the elevator," Al said.

"To the what?" Jan asked.

"This way," Al said, and led them to a pair of brushed chrome doors that met in the middle. He pushed a button in the wall next to them, and with the grumbling of loud machinery the doors slid open, revealing a room with padded walls and enough floor space for Al's automobile with some left over.

They went in and Al pushed another button, making the doors close with the same mechanical noise and then slam together. The room began to rise. Hunt's stomach went south while he went north.

"This is even worse than the automobile," Jan said as he leaned against the wall.

"Here," Hunt said when they got to the fifth floor. Al pushed another button and the chrome doors rumbled open.

"You fellows look a little green," Al said.

"A good color for a man from Venus," Jan said.

"What?" Andrew asked, surprised.

"Just get me out of here," Jan said. "I'll be fine."

Hunt led them along the main corridor until he stopped in front of a door just like the hundreds of other doors they'd passed; the number 5276 was stenciled onto it in black paint. "Here," he said again. His percepticon light was flickering as fast as a hummingbird's wing. Using a different key on his ring, Al clicked open the hanging lock and lifted it off the strike bar holding the door closed.

Inside, storage space 5276 was almost as big as Mr. Thrash's dining room and the walls were made of cinderblock bricks. It was empty except for one thing—Dr. Eignbergen's time machine stood in the middle of the room, lonely as the last rose of summer.

To Hunt the time machine still looked confusing, with its complex collection of long thin silver rods seemingly stuck any which-way into a glowing sphere in the center of a cubical frame. Some of the rods still didn't seem quite real.

Al cozied up to the machine and studied the controls. Hunt, Jan, and Andrew bunched up behind him, looking around him and over his shoulder—close but as impersonal as commuters on public transportation. Andrew giggled nervously. Nobody told him not to.

"Does it look familiar?" Jan asked.

"Close enough," Al assured him. He grabbed rods at the corners of the array and twisted them, causing indicators to appear, floating over the top of the frame. Lights began to move at the center of the sphere. Al held his hands above the rods and wiggled his fingers like a concert pianist about to come down hard on the first chord of a romantic ditty by Beethoven. "Where to?" he asked.

Silence gathered in the big empty room, in the enormous oppressive building, until it sounded like thunder in Hunt's ears. Then, far away, Hunt heard one of the light tubes buzzing. Behind him, Andrew or Jan shuffled his feet nervously.

"Let's go back to where we started," Hunt suggested, "back to the *Heinlein* a few seconds after we left. We'll have to awaken Dr. Eignbergen, but he'll be there. He might be able to help. And we'll be able to call out the System Guard police—if the System Guard still exists."

Al began to adjust the rods while watching the numbers on his gauges; Hunt could see that most of them were set close to zero. Soon the lights inside the sphere settled down into a small but realistic image.

"That's the storage bay," Jan exclaimed.

A blue bubble grew out of the nest of rods until it surrounded the machine, then surrounded all four of them. Suddenly it exploded like a burst balloon.

CHAPTER 16

ANDREW'S FUTURE

Hunt sat up and shook his head. Nearby, Jan, Al, and Andrew were doing the same. They were in the storage bay of what looked like the *Heinlein*.

"Freddy," Hunt called.

"Here, Raymond," Freddy answered, the voice of the ship's computer seeming to come from nowhere and everywhere, as usual. Hunt was pleased to hear it again. Freddy's voice confirmed they were aboard the *Heinlein*.

"How long have we been gone?"

"Gone, Raymond?" It was not possible for Freddy to sound confused, but he was able to ask questions.

"You know. The time machine went away and then it came back."

"I understand. No more than a few seconds."

"Good shooting, Al," Jan said.

"Miss Garley and Mr. Thrash could be here any minute," Andrew said, sounding worried.

"They might," Hunt said. "But just because they left aboard the time machine shortly after you arrived doesn't mean they'll be here any time soon. Or they might have already been here for months. What do you say, Al?"

Al frowned and pulled on an earlobe. "Time's funny stuff. Everything might depend on how the machine was adjusted when it arrived back in the nineteen-fifties, and how that Andrew—the one who had been through the cycle—handled the situation."

They all looked at Andrew.

"I don't know," he said, looking bewildered.

"Don't worry," Hunt assured him. "You will by the time we're done with you." Hunt clapped him on the shoulder. "Freddy," Hunt called, "would you please whip up a first year cadet uniform for Andrew?"

"Of course, Raymond. Show him to the clothier."

"Jan, will you do the honors?" Hunt asked.

Jan nodded, and grinning, led Andrew out of the bay.

"That might be all you need to convince him to open his flying school," Al said when they were gone.

"It might. But we're going to show him around, too. I don't want to take any chances. Come on, let's go surprise Dr. Eignbergen."

"I suppose we have time. If you have a time machine, you have all the time in the world."

They floated up the anti-grav tube to the personnel level and Hunt knocked on the door of the doctor's cabin. "Come in," the doctor called, sounding a little groggy.

When Hunt and Al went into the cabin, Dr. Eignbergen was sitting on the edge of his bunk rubbing his face. What there was of his hair was a mess. He'd obviously been napping. When he saw Al, all the sleep drained out of him. He suddenly looked wide awake – and surprised, just as they'd expected.

"Al?" he asked.

"It's me, Doc. Big as life and twice as natural."

"You found your way back."

"It's a long story."

"I'd like very much to hear it."

"All the time in the world, Al," Hunt reminded him.

That seemed to please both Al and the doctor. Al sat down in the single visitor's chair while the doctor got a small recording device from his flat case and set it up on a table that folded down from the wall.

"Do you know how long you've been gone, in my subjective time?" Dr. Eignbergen asked.

"No idea," Al said. "But I've been back in the nineteen-fifties for a few years, my time."

"Fair enough," the doctor said. "Please start at the beginning."

"You gentlemen won't be needing me," Hunt said. "If you want anything, ask Freddy."

Neither Al nor the doctor responded to Hunt. They just contemplated each other across the space between them—and maybe across the time between them, too. Hunt left them and walked to his cabin, where he found Jan and Andrew. Andrew was now wearing the dusty blue uniform of a first year cadet, and was nearly bursting out of it with pleasure.

"I see you're wearing a clean uniform," Hunt said to Jan.

"Why should Andrew be the only one who looks good?" Jan asked.

"Freddy," Hunt said into the air, "how long would it take you to clean me up and spray on a clean uniform?"

"If you're in a hurry, Raymond, three or four minutes."

"I think we can spare that," Jan said. "Andrew and I can probably find something to talk about."

Hunt went into the refresher, and Freddy worked him over with his magic waves and particles. He felt more clean, energetic, and alive with each passing moment.

When Freddy was done bathing him, he sprayed Hunt with a new uniform.

Feeling better than he had in days, Hunt went back into the cabin in time to hear Jan make a suggestion. "I don't suppose you're hungry, having had that big dinner two hundred years ago," he said.

"Yeah," Andrew said, rubbing his sleeve, as if still overwhelmed by the uniform. "I mean no. I mean you're right. I'm not hungry. Will you show me the ship?"

"Of course. Come on," Hunt said. He'd been about to suggest it himself. Jan ambled along after them.

They started with the galley just to get it over with, and from there, they went down to the power deck, a level full of blocky machines, levers, switches, big round instruments, and a constant gentle hum. Jan explained how the ship generated its power, and what made it go. Andrew looked at all the equipment hungrily, like a kid in a toy store.

"Don't touch anything," Jan advised Andrew. "We could end up in bits scattered all across this quadrant."

Andrew looked disappointed. "All right," he agreed with a sigh.

"Let's go up to the control deck," Hunt said. "There are some things I want to show you."

As Hunt, Jan, and Andrew rose to the top of the ship, Hunt thought of all the things that still needed to be done. They would start by showing Andrew the wonders of the future, and what his flying school would grow into. Soon after that, the five of them would need to talk things over, make a plan. Hunt was anxious to begin. Something could always go wrong. The sooner Ms. Garley and Mr. Thrash were in a place where they could do no harm, the better he'd like it.

When they reached the control deck, Hunt sat Andrew down in an acceleration couch. Fascinated by the universe in the astrogation sphere, Andrew leaned forward, his eyes big.

"The astrogation sphere projects in three-D," Hunt said. "You can walk all around it and see what's inside from any angle."

"Gosh," Andrew exclaimed. "This is better than television."

"Freddy," Hunt said, "show us what our course would look like if we could get to Earth in three minutes."

A green line shot from the center of the sphere and curved off toward the outer surface. Soon the Earth slid into the sphere and the green line circled the planet, going into orbit around it.

"That's pretty good, Hunt," Jan said. "I didn't know the sphere could to that."

"It's in the astrogation and command field manual," Hunt assured him. "Freddy, now show us the same thing from the point of view of the ship, this time all the way to touch-down at the Academy field."

Suddenly, the sphere became a front port. At first nothing much moved. The stars were too far away to change noticeably over so short a distance. Then the Earth, a big blue and green ball wrapped in clouds, entered the view and slowed as the ship approached it. Andrew held tight to the arms of his acceleration couch.

The ship dived through the clouds and flipped over, turning its tail toward the planetary surface. The sky brightened from star-spattered black to purple to hazy blue. The three looked up at the clouds they had just descended through.

"Let's have some sound, Freddy," Jan suggested.

Suddenly the room was filled with the thunder of the ship's engines laboring to set the ship down easy. The ship slowed, the view in the sphere shook once, and the thunder faded to nothing as the ship touched down.

"Wow," Andrew said, trying to catch his breath.

"Show us around the Academy, Freddy," Hunt said. "Start with the administration building."

"Yes, Raymond," Freddy said.

The administration building was a large imposing structure that looked as if it had been built from white marble blocks by ancient Greeks who had access to modern engineering methods—with columns as big as the redwood trees Hunt had seen, and a pediment carved with events from Academy history. Parts of the building seemed to hover without any support at all. The sphere took them from administration to the science building to the more modern command building. Between the buildings were wide lawns and any alien flora from around the solar system that could survive in Earthly conditions. A variety of humans and aliens strolled from building to building or lounged casually on the lawns. In some instances it was difficult to tell the flora from the fauna.

"Where are the ships?" Andrew asked. "I want to see the ships."

Jan chuckled. "I knew we'd get to that eventually," he said.

"Show us the ships, Freddy," Hunt requested.

The viewpoint moved quickly along paths of stone from many worlds and eventually came to the Academy terminus. It was a building even larger than administration, and it gave the impression of being a bird in flight. The viewpoint moved around behind it, and they saw a field full of spaceships. Andrew could do nothing but gape: some of the ships stood on fins, others lay on the on the ground like giant well-sharpened pencils on skids. Some were stubby, and others were tall and slender. As they watched, one of the slender ships was suddenly enveloped in purple fire that crackled and rumbled. In seconds the ship rose, seemed to punch a hole in the sky, and was gone.

For a long time Andrew just stared at the panorama. When he spoke again, it was softly, as if he were afraid to break the mood. "Which one looks like our ship?" he asked.

"Let's have a closer look at one of the Crockett class ships," Hunt said.

Immediately the viewpoint zoomed in on one of the stubbier ships resting on fins. "Just like the *Heinlein*," Jan assured Andrew.

"Let's go there," he demanded excitedly. "I want to see everything for real, not on television."

Jan watched Hunt, curious to see how he would explain.

"It will take three weeks for us to get to Earth," Hunt told Andrew.

"That's not very long," Andrew said, but sounding less than certain.

"It isn't, not really," Hunt said. "But Dr. Eignbergen and Al will be busy debriefing each other the whole time. There won't be much for any of us to do."

Andrew made a determined face.

"All right," Hunt said, "look at it this way. Do you know why I showed you all this?"

"I guarantee you it was not just out of the goodness of our hearts," Jan confided.

"It probably has something to do with Miss Garley and Mr. Thrash."

"That's right. I wanted to show you the System Guard Academy so you would see what grew out of your flying school."

"What flying school?"

"You'll find out," Jan said.

Andrew thought about that for a moment. "You're kidding," he said.

"No," Hunt said. "I wouldn't kid you if I could. I just wanted to show you that starting the flying school was more important than joining Mr. Thrash's acting company. I may have shown you too much of the future already; you may already be influenced beyond salvaging."

"No, no. I'll be all right."

"You have no idea," Jan told him.

Andrew mulled through that. "I guess you're right," he admitted.

"But that isn't all," Hunt continued. "At the Academy your picture is everywhere, old photographs in recordings, paintings on walls, even a statue or two. What do you think would happen if people begin to recognize you?"

"I don't know."

"I know," Jan said. "You'd become a celebrity. Even seeing as little as you already have, you will go back to your own time a different person. The longer you stay here, the more experiences you have, the more different you will become. You won't just be influenced, you'll be corrupted."

Andrew seemed on the verge of tears.

"None of that," Hunt admonished him.

Andrew sniffled and bucked up. "What happens next then?"

"That's better," Hunt said. "Three weeks from now, you and Al will have to return to the past together and arrive in the game room shortly before we escape through the secret panel. Garley and Thrash will not know that you just returned from the future. I'm hoping you'll have the opportunity to reset the time machine before they enter the game room. You can tell them that we forced Al to help Jan and me to escape – which, in a sense, is true. Thrash already knows about the secret panels, so this may not be much of a surprise. We'll have to rough Al up a little, just to make our story convincing."

Al smiled grimly at that.

"Garley and Thrash will take the time machine to the future. After they leave, all you have to do is go home with your parents and let nature take its course."

"Neither Thrash nor Garley know how to operate the time machine," Al reminded Hunt. "How can you be sure they'll get here at the right moment or at all?"

"It's a calculated risk," Hunt said. "For one thing, they'll have a little help. Unknown to them, Andrew will have set the machine to arrive just in time for them to be arrested by the System Guard police. For another, Garley is a gutsy woman who wants something. If she doesn't take herself and Thrash to the future, she will not be able to destroy the Academy."

"But still—" Andrew began.

"But still," Hunt interrupted, "it's a chance we have to take. Or took. All right?"

"I guess," Andrew said slowly.

"All right, then," Hunt said. "Sorry, but you'd better put on the clothes you arrived in."

After Andrew changed back into his original clothes, Hunt and Jan took him to Dr. Eignbergen's cabin, where the doctor and Al were still engaged in heavy conversation. "This is incredible," Dr. Eignbergen said. "We've barely begun."

Hunt explained their problem, and that they needed Dr. Eignbergen's expertise to adjust the time machine properly. He agreed immediately. Hunt suspected that he enjoyed doing these little tricks with his invention.

They strolled along the corridor, then dropped back to the storage bay, where the time machine still waited for them.

"Three weeks?" Dr. Eignbergen asked again just to make sure.

"Three weeks exactly," Jan assured him. "Meanwhile you and Al can continue your conversation. Andrew would just be bored on the ship. So we're sending him three weeks into the future, allowing him to skip to the exciting stuff."

Andrew smiled and looked embarrassed.

"And then," Hunt said, "Three weeks from now, when Andrew returns, with only a few seconds having passed for him, "you will show Andrew how to set the machine so Garley and Thrash will arrive here on the ship shortly after Andrew and Al leave for the 1950s, just in time to meet up with the System Guard police."

But for now, Andrew joined the doctor at the time machine and watched carefully as he adjusted the rods. Soon the storage bay appeared in the nest where the rods met. It was odd seeing the same scene on the machine's screen as the one around them. Of course, the scene on the machine was three weeks in the future of the one where they all stood. Hunt imagined members of the System

Guard police hiding behind cargo crates, ready to jump out when Garley and Thrash appeared.

"Ready?" Hunt asked.

"Sure," Andrew said, though Hunt didn't think he looked or sounded ready. Still, he knew that Andrew would never be any readier.

Andrew approached the time machine and for a moment, stared at it as if he had not seen it before. Then he adjusted the rods. A moment later the blue bubble grew around him. A moment after that, he and the machine were gone.

CHAPTER 17

THREE WEEKS PLUS

"I guess the kid will be all right," Jan said. "I was getting so I kind of liked him."

"He'll be fine," Hunt said. "From his viewpoint, he won't be gone longer than a few seconds." He frowned at Dr. Eignbergen.

"What's eating you, Cadet Hunt?" the doctor asked, as if accusing him of something not very serious.

"I was just thinking about what I told Andrew before he left. I suggested that he may have seen too much of the future already, that he may have already been influenced beyond salvaging, that the universe might change for us—for himself most certainly—and not necessarily for the better."

"We're still here," Jan pointed out. "We're still wearing Academy uniforms."

Hunt kept looking at Dr. Eignbergen.

"Perhaps he was influenced just enough," the doctor suggested.

"I don't understand," Hunt said.

"Perhaps Andrew started the flying school and created the Academy *because* he saw the future. Maybe in our own past Andrew was corrupted the same way. Maybe without the corruption there would be no Academy."

"I told you time was funny stuff," Al said.

"We believed you," Jan said. "But maybe we didn't believe you *enough*."

Into the thoughtful silence that followed, Dr. Eignbergen dropped a suggestion that Al join him in his cabin. "We still have a lot to talk about," he said. The two of them walked eagerly out of the storage bay, already discussing time travel and how it applied to life in the twentieth century.

"That takes care of them," Jan said. "What will we do with our three weeks?"

"We both have studying to do. And you can continue your experiments in the galley if you want to. Personally, I'm going to call the System Guard police and suggest they meet us when we get to Earth."

Jan nodded and headed back to the power deck, walking with his usual jaunty gait.

Hunt went up to the control deck where he spent some time confirming the *Heinlein's* location in the astrogation sphere. Everything came out even, which he knew it would; Freddy rarely if ever made mistakes.

"Freddy," Hunt said, "get me the System Guard police."

"Immediately, Raymond."

Hunt clawed his way through three secretaries, and finally connected with Captain Norwalk, a gruff old guy with the drooping face of an unhappy bulldog. He looked like a man who would have trouble believing in time travel. Hunt explained the situation as best he could, and asked for help from the System Guard.

Norwalk glanced at something to the right of the sphere at his end. Whatever he saw there did not please him. "I see that Commandant Cassidy ordered you and Cadet Jan to pick up Dr. Eignbergen. The orders don't say anything about the police getting involved, or about time travel, for that matter."

Hunt sighed. "Yes, sir," he said. "It's kind of complicated. However, if you want to hear my complete story in detail, I would be delighted to tell it to you. I have plenty of time."

"I'm sorry to say that I do not. But on the off chance you've evaluated the situation correctly, we'll send a few officers out to meet your ship on the date and at the place you suggest. I hope the trouble we take is worthwhile."

"It will be, sir," Hunt said.

"Time travel," Captain Norwalk harrumphed, and broke the connection.

Hunt thought about calling Commandant Cassidy and telling her what was going on. He would probably get a more satisfactory reception than he'd received from Captain Norwalk, but at last Hunt decided that bothering Cassidy right now was pointless. She would listen with her small, calm smile and then tell Hunt to keep doing what he was doing until doing it no longer made any sense. Hunt wondered how sympathetic he himself would be if somebody else told him the sort of tale he was spinning.

* * * *

It was a long three weeks. When he wasn't cooking, Jan stayed on the power deck, reading dials and making small unnecessarily adjustments while Hunt kept to the control deck studying astrogation and command theory. Freddy could have done what Jan was doing and made most of the decisions that Hunt made, but the computer was programmed to give the humans aboard the ship as much freedom to make their own decisions as possible.

Al and Dr. Eignbergen usually emerged from the doctor's cabin only at meal times. Jan made a lot of Venusian dishes, and both Al and the doctor were willing to try most of them. Hunt also attempted to keep an open mind. (Only Jan would eat the Mud Slug Pasta. The rest of them thought the stuff was still alive. Jan claimed it was not. "I saw it move," Hunt maintained.) A few times the doctor joined Hunt for a game of checkers and more often than not the doctor won. Al was his usual jovial self.

As they approached Earth, tension aboard the ship increased like the tightening of a violin string. Would Andrew return and pick up Al before Garley and Thrash arrived? Would the police turn up at the right moment? Would they be able to stop Garley and Thrash? Had Hunt screwed up everything by inviting Andrew to the future?

* * * *

The day came when Andrew was due to arrive.

Though they had not discussed meeting early, Hunt, Jan, Al, and Dr. Eignbergen found themselves gathered in the storage bay a whole hour beforehand. It wouldn't make Andrew arrive any sooner, but after three weeks, waiting in the storage bay was something new to do, and they couldn't help themselves. A watched pot always boils—eventually.

"How long until the System Guard police get here?" Dr. Eignbergen asked.

"Freddy," Hunt called, "answer the doctor's question."

"Approximately fifty-seven minutes," Freddy said.

"I suppose that'll give Andrew time to return and pick up Al," Jan said.

"Time and a little over," Dr. Eignbergen said. "Just enough for the police to be in place when Ms. Garley and Mr. Thrash get here."

"A split-second operation," Jan remarked. "Just like you said."

"I hope so," Hunt said.

Hunt didn't see when it happened, but when he looked again at the open space in the center of the storage bay, the blue time bubble had already appeared. As it grew they all stood up from the crates where they had been sitting. A moment later the bubble burst silently, leaving Andrew and the time machine in the middle of the deck.

"Didn't it work?" Andrew asked as he looked around him.

"It worked just fine," Hunt said.

"Oh, sure," Andrew said as if he understood what had happened. Maybe he did. Time travel was nothing new to him now.

"Doctor, would you show Andrew how to set the machine so it'll transport Garley and Thrash here at the right moment to meet the System Guard police?"

Dr. Eignbergen nodded and manipulated the rods while Andrew and Al watched. He moved the rods into random positions and invited Andrew to reset them correctly. He had Andrew do it three or four times just to make sure he had the hang of it. As Hunt had hoped, on each occasion the process took less than a minute.

"All right," Dr. Eignbergen said, "I'm convinced."

Hunt and Jan agreed with him. Hunt knew that Andrew could practice forever, and he still wouldn't be sure that Andrew would be able to do the trick.

Dr. Eignbergen adjusted the rods one more time, and soon the game room in Mr. Thrash's mansion appeared in the center of the machine. "All right, gentlemen," he said, and backed away.

"Wait a minute," Hunt said. "We have one more thing to take care of, though I'm sorry to say it. We'll have to injure you a little, Al."

"I know," Al said, his expression tight but trying to be pleasant. "I was about to suggest it myself." He looked at Andrew. "It's the only way to convince Mr. Thrash that I tried to prevent these two from escaping."

Andrew nodded, but he didn't look happy.

"Give it to 'em, Hunt," Jan said.

Hunt waved his finger over the cuff of his uniform shirt, turning the blast of his weapon down to minimum.

"Go ahead, Hunt," Al said. "We don't have all day."

"Sure we do," Jan responded, and pointed meaningfully at the time machine.

"Cut the comedy," Al said, gritting his teeth.

Hunt blasted him in the shoulder with a shaft of purple light, blowing Al's shirt apart, and setting it to glowing at the open edges with orange sparks that crawled like luminous worms. Inside the shirt Hunt was disgusted to see wet blackened skin.

"Thanks," Al said, but he winced when he said it.

"Anything else?" Dr. Eignbergen asked.

"No," Hunt said and turned away. He had done the right thing, the only thing possible, but that didn't make him feel any better. He stood next to Jan, staring at the deck.

Andrew and Al crowded around the machine. "Go ahead," Al said.

To Hunt's surprise, Andrew turned to where he and Jan were standing together. "This is it, isn't it?" Andrew said. "I'll never see you fellows again."

"That's right," Hunt said, feeling as sorry as Andrew sounded.

Andrew solemnly shook hands with Hunt and Jan and the doctor, then looked as if he were going to say something else. But he turned back to the machine and quickly adjusted the final rod. The blue bubble grew and burst, taking Andrew, Al, and the machine with it.

Less than five seconds later Freddy told them that the police were ready to come aboard. They were sending across a snake and would soon be making their way through it.

"Here we go," Jan said.

CHAPTER 18

HERE WE GO

The clamps attached themselves against the hull of the *Heinlein* with sharp taps and one loud metallic bang after another. Jan went to open the inner door of the airlock.

To Hunt's distress, the moment Jan was gone a small blue bubble appeared in the middle of the storage bay. "We're in for it now," he said and ducked behind a crate from which he watched the blue bubble grow.

Dr. Eignbergen crouched next to Hunt.

The bubble burst. Garley and Thrash looked around quickly, as if they expected to be ambushed. They were each in the clothes they had been wearing on the night of the big dinner—more than three weeks ago for Hunt, only minutes ago for Garley and Thrash—Garley in her Amethyst Queen outfit, and Thrash in his tuxedo.

Garley recovered her composure first, of course, having grown up in the future. "See?" she said as she smiled broadly, "I told you I could do it." Thrash complimented her, but he still looked worried. Garley ran to the storage bay's auxiliary door and waved her hand over the control that opened it.

"You might as well come out, Cadet Hunt," Mr. Thrash said. "I see your foot sticking out from behind that crate." Hunt motioned to Dr. Eignbergen to stay where he was, then stood up to find that Mr. Thrash was pointing a weapon at him. Hunt identified it as a twentieth century pistol that threw small projectiles.

"I hope you're not planning to fire that in here," Hunt casually remarked. "If it makes a hole in the outer wall of the ship we're all dead."

"Oh, please," Mr. Thrash said. "I doubt whether your ship is made of aluminum foil."

"I guess you know what you're doing," Hunt said. He wondered what was keeping the police.

Seconds later he found out. The bay's main door slid open, and about a dozen military police officers rushed in, their integrated weapons at the ready. They fired at Garley and Thrash, but by that time the two were had fled out the storage bay's auxiliary door. Shafts of purple light splashed off the bulkhead where the two scoundrels had been the moment before.

"What—" one of the officers began.

Hunt interrupted. "I'll explain when there's time," he said. "Jan, help these officers find our friends." Nobody knew the ship better than Jan.

Jan rushed across the bay, leading the group out the auxiliary door, which by now had slid open all the way.

Dr. Eignbergen stood up behind his crate. "Will the officers get them?" he asked Hunt.

Hunt shrugged. And with the shrug came an idea. When he explained what he had in mind, the doctor didn't understand at first and Hunt had to explain the idea in more detail.

"Ah," the doctor said, and he went to the time machine and opened a small door in its side, down where the rods joined. He hummed as he poked around inside—a man enjoying his work.

"Freddy?" Hunt called.

"Yes, Raymond," Freddy answered.

"Where are our two fugitives from justice?"

"In the spacesuit changing chamber," Freddy reported, "moving toward sickbay."

"Start closing doors behind them as they move around the ship. I want you to help Jan and the officers herd them back here to the storage bay."

"Yes, Raymond." Immediately the auxiliary door of the storage bay slid closed.

Hunt lifted his sleeve and made the appropriate motions over the cuff. "Jan?"

"We're kinda busy here, Hunt," Jan said, sounding a trifle out of breath as he trotted along. "I think they're headed for the control deck."

"See if you can turn them back toward the storage bay. I've asked Freddy to help you."

"Why? I mean why do you want them in the storage bay?"

"The doc and I will have a little surprise for them."

Jan chuckled. "Aye aye, cadet captain," he said.

"All ready here," Dr. Eignbergen said.

Hunt nodded. Each of them settled onto a crate. "How are we doing, Freddy?" Hunt asked.

"They are headed your way," the computer said. "Longwood and the police officers are not far behind them."

"Hide," Hunt said to the doctor. "We don't want to frighten them off."

Hunt and the doctor crouched behind their crates again, taking care that no body parts showed. In the corridor outside the main storage bay door, shouting and the sound of running grew louder, like an approaching storm.

Garley and Thrash ran into the big room, glancing around, expecting to be attacked from any and all sides. Behind them, Jan and the police were approaching quickly.

"The time machine," Garley said as she crossed to it, and studied it as quickly as she could. "It's our only way out."

"We could end up fighting dinosaurs," Thrash retorted.

"We really have no other choice," Garley shot back. "Come on."

Thrash joined her at the machine, and Garley adjusted the rods until the game room in Mr. Thrash's mansion appeared on the tiny ball where the rods joined.

Jan stood in the doorway. "Hold it right there," he ordered as he pointed his weapon at them.

Garley blew him a kiss, then twisted a rod on the machine. A blue bubble appeared around the machine, then grew large enough to engulf both her and Thrash. Hunt stood up from behind his crate, and motioned for Jan and the police officers to lower their weapons.

Unlike the bubble's behavior when it traveled in time, it now grew only so large and then stopped. Inside, Garley was still smiling, and Thrash seemed calm. Neither of them moved—no blinking, no breathing. Jan and the police officers gathered around.

"What happened?" Jan asked.

"Do you remember what Dr. Eignbergen told us about his ideas for preserving food using some kind of time-travel gimmick?"

"So?" Jan asked.

"So, observe," Hunt said, and gestured toward the blue bubble. "Two sides of beef."

"They look like statues," Jan said. "How long can they stay in there like that?"

"How long to do you want them to stay like that?" the doctor asked.

"Just till we get them into a brig back on Earth," one of the police officers said.

"That should be no problem," the doctor said. "I'll need some help carrying them and their time bubble."

"That's no problem either," the policeman said, and gestured to his crew. Four of the officers stepped forward. With a grunt from each, they lugged the whole package from the room. Dr. Eignbergen strolled after them.

"Welcome to Earth," Jan said.

"At last," Hunt remarked.

CHAPTER 19

TIME IS FUNNY STUFF

With the usual thunder and shudder they landed the *Heinlein* smartly on the Academy field. They were met just outside the blast bowl by a cart driven by a lieutenant with a chest full of ribbons. If she was a desk jockey, she had not always been such. The System Guard didn't give ribbons for filling out forms.

"You're Hunt and Jan?" the lieutenant asked.

"Yes, sir," Hunt said.

"Get in," the lieutenant ordered. "Commandant Cassidy is waiting for you."

Even Jan knew this was no time for brash remarks. He and Hunt boarded the cart and it bobbed a little on its anti-gravity cushion. Seconds later they were rushing across the field to the admin building with the wind in their hair—a pleasant sensation after spending so many weeks in the can. Hunt was not surprised by the special treatment. Captain Norwalk had probably reported his version of Hunt's story to the Commandant. Cassidy would not believe everything Norwalk told her, but the information would be enough to stimulate her curiosity. Hunt and Jan still had a lot of explaining to do.

The cart floated up the steps of the administration building, between the white marble columns, and into the lobby—an enormous room which contained a crater in which a full-size diorama of the Eagle landing on the moon was presented. Tourists and first year cadets leaned on the railing and pointed out features of historical interest to each other in the three-dimensional exhibit far below. The lieutenant drove them past the crater without a second glance.

Still riding in the cart, the three of them rose to the fifth floor and down a hallway hung with three-dimensional moving pictures of famous graduates saluting, or grinning up from the machinery they were fixing, or dropping in armored battle suits toward hostile alien worlds—their sweaty faces grim, determined, and in many cases, needing a shave. Between the graduates were small, old-fashioned paintings of airplanes and spaceships that hadn't flown in decades. A few carts went the other way, carrying high-ranking Guard officers.

The lieutenant pulled up in front of a door like many of the others and invited Hunt and Jan to enter.

"Aren't you coming?" Jan asked.

"The Commandant is waiting for you," the lieutenant reminded them flatly. Hunt knocked, received a grunt from beyond the door and the two of them went in. They never did learn the lieutenant's name.

Commandant Cassidy was a hefty, gray-haired woman with an open, friendly face. The two cadets saluted. Behind her was a big window looking out over a pine forest that was probably a recording of a place where the Commandant went on vacation. Birds flew from branch to branch while squirrels ran up and down the trunks, all the while keeping up a constant chittering conversation that was piped into the office. The Commandant sat behind a glassite desk stroking projections of papers with her big, knobby hands, moving them around. When the projections were organized as she liked them, she touched a control and they disappeared, leaving behind a featureless transparent surface.

"Come in, gentlemen," the Commandant said as she returned their salute. Her words were more of an invitation than an order. "Sit down. You'll be here a while."

Hunt and Jan sat down. Despite the Commandant's friendly attitude, Hunt was nervous. He had no idea what Cassidy was really thinking.

"As you probably know, Ms. Bernadette Garley and Mr. Christopher Thrash are currently in the academy brig. They deny most of what you told Captain Norwalk."

"It's all true," Jan said. "Ask Dr. Eignbergen."

"Our science experts are speaking to the doctor right now. But as you might imagine, he has a peculiarly rigorous point of view, with more of an interest in how well his machine worked than in any adventures you two may have had. Besides, you two are the only ones who were in on the affair right from the beginning. I'd like to hear the story from you. Why don't you go first, Cadet Hunt?"

Jan snuggled back into his chair, knit his fingers across his middle, and smiled at Hunt.

Hunt ignored him, then concentrated on telling the Commandant how they had rescued Garley, become involved with Thrash back in the middle of the twentieth century, and learned of Garley's plan to prevent the System Guard Academy from being established by Andrew Gordon. He recounted the attack on Carnival Town and the dinner at Mr. Thrash's mansion that had eventually led to their returning to their own time.

"I guess we did all right," Hunt said, winding up his story. "The Academy is still here."

"That would be a logical conclusion," the Commandant agreed. She looked at Jan, who had become very relaxed indeed while Hunt spoke. "Mr. Jan?"

Jan jumped. "Yes, sir."

"If it's not too much trouble, let's hear your version."

"Yes, sir." Jan sat up straight and told pretty much the same story as had Hunt, except for a few minor details.

When Jan had finished, Commandant Cassidy nodded. She hadn't taken any notes, but Hunt did not doubt that every word spoken in the office had been recorded. Cassidy and her experts would later pour both stories through a fine mesh. Hunt supposed that he and Jan would have to tell their stories again anyway, next time in a courtroom, to determine what would happen to Garley and Thrash.

Commandant Cassidy seemed to have gone into a private reverie, looking straight ahead at the empty space between the two cadets, her hands flat on her desk. She shook her head and seemed to awaken. "Oh, and by the way," she said. "I almost forgot. Harvey, my computer, tells me that he's been holding a private message for you two for over two hundred years."

"For us?" Hunt asked. As far as he knew, the possible identities of the sender were limited.

The Commandant asked Harvey to present the letter.

"Right away, sir," Harvey said.

Immediately a layer of black marks rose through the glassite like a school of meteorites tumbling through space. When the marks reached the surface of the desk they solidified into a rectangular sheet with words on it. Cassidy handed the sheet to Hunt. Jan tried to look over Hunt's shoulder, but their chairs were too far apart.

"I assume that is a private communication," Commandant Cassidy said. "You may read it at your leisure."

"Thank you, sir," Hunt said as he folded the letter and slid it into a pocket.

"I believe that will be all for now, gentlemen."

"Thank you, sir," Hunt said. He and Jan stood, saluted, and left as quickly as they could. They descended to the lobby level, and Jan followed Hunt to the rail at the edge of the Eagle diorama. Hunt pulled the letter from his pocket and read out loud:

Dear Hunt and Jan,

By the time you read this I will be long dead. But I wanted you to know how things turned out after I returned to my own time. When Al and I arrived in the game room, I had just enough opening to reset the time machine as we had planned before Miss Garley and Mr. Thrash entered. The injury you gave Al seemed to convince them that he was still on their side, but beyond that they were not interested in him. Mr. Thrash was not very interested in me either, though he did suggest to Miss Garley that murdering me right then and there would just complicate matters. He also wondered where (when?) the machine had come from. Miss Garley didn't know either, but fortunately for all of us, she was too eager to get going to consider the possibilities. The next thing I knew, they had gone off in the time machine to pick up weapons from the future. You know better than I how successful they were. My parents and Mr. Llewelyn entered shortly thereafter. They had come to an agreement on how and when and for how much I was supposed to work on Space League. *Though Mr. Thrash never returned, the show continued, now run by Mr. Slippery Sam Pepper. But I really wasn't much of an actor. Flying was more my style. There is probably an official history of how my flying school became the System Guard Academy. In any case, it was a pleasure meeting you gentlemen, and being an important part of your past. I guess Dr. Eignbergen was right about how much I may have changed the future – just enough?*

Hot jets, clear ether, spaceman's luck,
Andrew Gordon

"Well, I'll be damned," Jan said. "What do you think that letter is worth?"

"Plenty, I suppose," Hunt said. "Assuming anybody we know was going to sell it."

Jan contemplated him for a moment. Then he nodded. "I suppose you want to donate it to the Academy."

"We'll probably have to after we read it at the big trial."

"Will we have to do that?"

Hunt shrugged. "Remember what Al said—time is funny stuff."